BRACED FOR HEARTACHE

MILLER FAMILY MEDICAL
BOOK 3

DAPHNE JAMES HUFF

Miller Family
MEDICAL ROMANCE

Braced For Heartache

DAPHNE JAMES HUFF

ONE

CLEMENTINE

With a flip of her hair and a sparkling smile, Clementine Miller waved. "Hi, Mark."

Her lips pulled down in a frown, and she rolled her eyes at herself in the bathroom mirror. No, that sounded too peppy.

She tried again, this time without the smile.

"Hello, Dr. Vickers."

Ugh, even worse. That made her sound boring and official. Like a regular colleague or even a client, which she most definitely did not want to be. Plus physical therapists didn't normally use the title *doctor*, so he'd know she was trying to impress him.

"Good morning." A smaller smile. "Lovely day, isn't it?"

There, that sounded natural, and the slight curl of her lips was definitely alluring, not deranged.

She let out a loud puff of air and buried her face in her hands, wishing she could sink into the checkerboard tile of her bathroom and disappear.

Clementine had a problem. She was in love with her boss, but he barely spoke to her beyond polite morning greetings and the occasional "any plans this weekend?" that she clung to like her cat clung to the living room curtains. If Mark hadn't noticed her by now, changing how she said hello to him wasn't going to make a difference.

The drip of the bathtub faucet was like a drill in her head, repeating the words over and over.

He doesn't care, he doesn't care, he doesn't care...

Except he might be at Jasper Creek's Fall Festival this weekend. When she mentioned it at work the day before, all of her colleagues sounded interested, including Mark. So if nothing else, she might get to talk to him outside of work for the first time. That was better than nothing, wasn't it?

After one final look in the mirror to check her hair, she headed into the living room. She grabbed her keys, gave her cat, Marbles, a scratch behind the ears while he devoured his breakfast, and headed out the door.

Maybe she didn't have to do anything for Mark to notice her. Maybe he'd realize on his own how wonderful she was.

That's about as likely as Anais letting go of control or Bastien letting someone help him.

A snort of self-deprecating laughter burst from her as she pulled out of her driveway. While others might go to their older siblings for help, in Clementine's case, they were the last people who she'd talk to about this. Anais and Bastien were twins, unalike in so many ways but eerily similar in giving opinions of how their three younger siblings should live their lives.

Shaking her head, Clementine turned left at the end of the road to start the short trip into the center of Jasper Creek to see her family—and hopefully her boss too.

The signs for the Fall Festival had been up for weeks, and it was finally opening day. Bastien usually ran things like this for the town almost entirely on his own, but he'd been taking things easy since his son was born a month ago. The first grandchild for their parents and Clementine's first nephew. She beamed just thinking about little Jamie, even more excited at the possibility of seeing him than running into Mark.

Clementine drove past and waved out the window to familiar couples who walked hand in hand. It was hard not to wonder how everyone managed to make love look so easy. Twenty-five and never been kissed wasn't something to be ashamed of, Clementine knew that, but it did make it harder to know where to even start.

Outgoing and popular in a way Clementine could only dream of being, her sister Dani didn't seem to have this problem. Guilt licked through Clementine's chest when she realized she was happy Dani wouldn't be at the festival. With her sister away at med school, it would mean one less distraction to worry about while she tried to catch and keep Mark's attention today.

The Fall Festival was in full swing by the time she found a parking spot and walked into the town square. This was the first year Clementine had been able to come to the festival since she'd finished physical therapy school, so she was really looking forward to it, and not just because of Mark. As usual, the booth for apple cider donuts had the longest line, and Carl, who ran the bakery, was trying his best to keep up without his daughter, Carly, with him. She was away at college like Eli, Clementine's younger brother.

Weaving through the crowds, Clementine waved when she saw two of her colleagues from the PT clinic. They exchanged small talk while her eyes scanned the crowd for Mark. It was unprofessional to have such a huge crush on him. She knew that. But she couldn't stop the way her heart beat faster whenever she saw the tall, smart, funny man who'd taken her on as an intern over the summer, then hired her full time at the end of her degree.

He probably didn't even realize what a big deal it was for her to have gotten a job like this right out of school. Working for such a large clinic that already had two locations was exactly what she needed to get the experience to open her own.

That was a "someday" dream, however. Her more immediate burning desire was to see Mark and talk to him, maybe even make him smile.

The telltale thump in her chest let her know he was in the vicinity somewhere.

"Oh hi, Mark." Melissa, one of her colleagues, waved and smiled, perfectly casual and genuine.

Sticky jealousy rippled through Clementine, but she tried her best to tamp it down. The older woman was a genuinely lovely person, married with two kids, who probably didn't even notice how attractive Mark was. Meanwhile, Clementine was having trouble staying upright.

"Hey, everyone. It's nice to see you all in regular clothes for once." Mark's deep chuckle almost brought Clementine to her knees. "I didn't even recognize you all without scrubs."

The others laughed as well, while all Clementine could manage was a small, strained upward tilt of her lips.

"It's just as cute as you said it would be, Clem." Mark turned his attention to her, and the intense jolt of his eyes on hers warred with the familiar flutter of annoyance at the terrible nickname. He'd used it on her first day as an intern, and everyone had started using it. Five months later, she still didn't have the courage to tell them how much she hated it.

Though it wasn't that bad when Mark was saying it in his deep, rumbling voice.

"So where should we start?" Now his attention was fully on her, and she wasn't sure where to look or what to do. Her eyes darted around as her heart ping-ponged in her chest.

Should she talk about the beer tent or the donuts? The costume parade or the jack-o'-lantern competition?

"Um, I think there's, I mean, if you go over that way..." Her arms flailed for a moment, then she gestured in two directions at once.

Three pairs of eyes were following her movements, and heat spread across her face. Sweat pooled under her arms despite the cool autumn breeze swirling around them. She dropped her hands to her sides. "It's fun. All fun."

Clementine shut her mouth with a snap and prayed the earth would open up and eat her.

"I'm sure it is." Mark's lips curled up in a smile, and he turned away from her, taking half of her heart with him.

One of her colleagues mentioned the donuts, and Mark's eyes lit up. "Should we all go get some?"

While the others nodded, panic zipped through her chest. She wanted to say yes, but what came out when she opened her mouth was, "I have to bathroom."

I have to bathroom? That's not even a complete sentence!

"Okay, we'll see you around." The three of them walked off without a backward glance at her.

Furious with herself, she stalked off into the crowd in the opposite direction. After all that practice, she'd blown it. Why was it so impossible to act normal around him? It shouldn't be this hard. Her sister Dani flirted with everyone, and none of her friends ever got tongue-tied around guys they liked. It was like everyone else had taken some one-day seminar and she'd been out sick that day.

It wasn't just that Mark was attractive and smart. He was such an inspiration to her, having started his own PT clinic only a few years ago in the suburbs of Denver and already expanding it to a second location in Jasper Creek. Her own family had owned Miller Family Medical for decades but had kept it small.

The smell of apple pie and fresh pumpkins floated in the cool air as she weaved her way around the booths, most of them the same now as when she was a kid. Clementine had always had bigger dreams than going to work for her family and staying in Jasper Creek, but she'd had faltering success so far in pursuing those dreams. Mark was everything she wanted, everything she wanted to be. If only she could manage to talk to him like a human, not a robot, then she might actually have a shot at the future she'd always pictured for herself.

"Minnie!"

At the sound of the family nickname she loved, she turned, and a wide smile spread across her face when she saw her brother Bastien and his wife Gabby. No practicing needed for this greeting. "There's my favorite nephew."

She scooped up the baby boy Bastien was holding. The future could wait when there were chubby baby cheeks that needed to be kissed.

"He's your only nephew," Bastien said with an eye roll, but there was a pleased grin on his face that had been there for the past year or so.

"For now." Clementine rocked Jamie in her arms, and he cooed appreciatively.

"I hope you don't expect another from me anytime soon." Bastien's wife, Gabby—the other reason for his now constant happiness—sidled up next to him, and he looped an arm around her. "This one barely lets us sleep."

"I think she may be referring to Anais." Dr. Austin Gibson appeared behind Gabby, a stuffed bear in one hand and cotton candy in the other.

The sight of the handsome doctor sent the usual flutter through Clementine's belly, but after three years of seeing him around Jasper Creek, she was almost—almost—used to his dazzling good looks. She was able to laugh and smile at his comment rather than crumple into a ball of nerves the way she used to back when he first started working for Miller Family Medical and she'd been the receptionist.

She just had to figure out how to act the same around Mark, then she'd be all set.

"I didn't mean Anais at all, but has she said something to you?" Clementine shifted her nephew from one shoulder to the other, keeping a gentle hand around his head to support his floppy baby neck.

Both Gabby and Bastien turned, just as eager for Austin's answer.

"No, but I think I recognize the signs." Austin handed off the bear to Bastien and the cotton candy to Gabby, whose eyes lit up as she tore into the sugary treat. Hands now free, he ticked off items on his fingers. "She's extremely grumpy, she's not eating in the morning, and she's obscenely competitive with her brother, so she has probably been trying since the second she found out Gabby was expecting. Likely even before."

Clementine bit back a smile. That last reason in particular was very Anais. The oldest Miller sibling was spectacular, but also a little scary in how smart and dedicated she was. If Anais wanted something, she was going to get it, one way or another.

Bastien nodded. "That definitely tracks. Good work, Gibson."

There was the smallest surprised raise of Austin's eyebrows before his face smoothed out to its typical handsomely confident smile. It reminded her of Mark's, except Austin had dimples.

"Are you going to be the one to ask if it's true?" Gabby gestured with her chin, and they all looked to see Anais approaching with her husband, Jackson. She did look grumpier than she usually did, but beautiful as always, her sleek, dark hair tucked under a cute wool hat that matched her boots.

Austin shook his head. "Absolutely not. I vote Clementine asks."

"What?" she squawked, and Jamie wriggled in protest at the sudden loud noise. Just as he started to snuffle in agitation, she handed him back to Bastien. "Oh, look at that, what a coincidence, auntie time is over and he's fussy."

This was her sign to leave the festival for the day. She'd embarrassed herself in front of her boss, and the last thing she needed was to feel even worse after interacting with her sister. Who she loved, of course, but Anais was somehow more intimidating now than she'd ever been growing up.

If Clementine had gone to med school, like Anais, then she could have slipped into the role of apprentice, asking her sister for advice on specialties and paths, gotten help studying, things like that. Instead, Clementine had forged her own path in physical therapy, which she was proud of but also anxious about.

She wasn't working at Miller Family Medical the way Millers had for generations. Dani and Eli would join Anais when they were done with school, and even Bastien was married to a nurse practitioner who worked there. She hadn't completely split from medicine, like Bastien, who was a teacher, but she wasn't a physician. Even though it's what she wanted for her life, it left her wondering where she fit in.

The answer was nowhere, and she didn't need the reminder today, not when she'd failed so spectacularly with Mark.

"I see a friend from high school." Heart pounding in her ears, Clementine waved in the opposite direction of Anais, where a mass of people was crowding around the display of carved pumpkins. "I'll catch up with everyone later."

They all nodded their goodbyes, though Austin was giving her a strange look. Halfway between curiosity and concern, his deep blue eyes were looking at her like he could see everything rushing through her head. Her heart gave an extra hard thump as she turned away from him and hurried off, planning to lose herself in the crowd before sneaking out of the festival.

Luckily, Austin couldn't actually read minds, or she'd be in real trouble.

Poking a finger underneath the dark sunglasses that shielded him from the brutal sun, Dr. Austin Gibson rubbed his eyes and wished he had remembered to put a bottle of water in his car. Now he'd have to wait until he was at the office since he didn't have time to go home.

Maybe he'd stop at Carl's Café instead. The thought of a few donuts and some coffee sounded a lot better than Anais's judgy stares while he sipped something in the break room. She'd been extra tetchy lately, and even if he was ninety-five percent sure he knew why and she was just waiting for the right moment to announce the happy news, he couldn't deal with her right now.

He pulled into the parking lot for Carl's Café and sighed. Everything had been feeling like too much lately to deal with. No, that was wrong. It was the opposite. Nothing was too much, and yet that was somehow just as overwhelming. It had been the same in those final weeks with Cassidy, before everything imploded. Things were too simple, too easy, too predictable.

Like Anais. They'd been friends for years, coworkers for almost three. So he knew exactly what she'd say if he walked in looking like he'd barely slept. He'd already heard countless times her thoughts on his choice of nighttime activities: that it wasn't the right way to deal with these inescapable feelings of loneliness that had taken hold when Cassidy broke up with him.

He could practically hear Anais's understanding but exasperated tone as he got out of the car and was met with the all-too-familiar stinging mix of a bright sun and wintry, early November wind.

It's been three years, Austin. It's time to move on.

Though apparently "move on" in Anais's world didn't mean showing every cute tourist who came through the Floodline bar just how much fun there was to be had. And escorting them back to their rental house was just the polite, welcoming, small-town thing to do, wasn't it?

Austin opened the door to the café and let a few people out. They smiled at him, recognizing him even with his sunglasses, just like he knew they would. Of course, he steered clear of dating anyone who actually lived in Jasper Creek. No sense making it awkward for someone at their next checkup if the doctor treating them had forgotten to call them back.

It had been months, however, since he'd spent a night with anyone, tourist or otherwise. What had been a distraction had become banal, just like everything else. He hadn't been to the Floodline in weeks even though Matt and Carter Hayes, the cousins who owned it, kept bugging him to stop by.

No, if he was tired today, it was because he'd been up all night finishing a puzzle—the only thing that seemed to keep his spinning mind occupied these days. But once he'd started, of course he'd had to finish. Not that Anais would believe that.

The last time he'd had any kind of real fun was when Gabby had joined the practice the previous year as an NP. Making sure she ended up happy—even if it was with Bastien Miller, of all people—had been wonderfully entertaining. Between her and Anais and Matt and Carter, he had plenty of friends. They had their own lives though, and there was only so much meddling he could do before that got boring too.

Just as he walked into the café, his phone buzzed. He swiped to see a message from his sister.

MOM & DAD ARE BOOKING A NEW PLACE THIS YEAR AND NEED A HEAD COUNT. CONFIRMING IT'LL JUST BE YOU?

A familiar snap of loneliness clamped over his chest. He couldn't take a friend to his family's annual holiday ski trip. He'd already gotten way too much pity from his family when Cassidy dumped him. Bringing a friend on the trip would make it ten times worse. It would essentially be a declaration that he'd given up entirely on finding love. Which, even if he had, he didn't need to announce to his family.

Deciding to send his disappointing reply later, after he'd had his caffeine, he joined the line at the counter, reveling in the wind snaking through the door whenever it opened. The cold at his back was welcome, and not just because it kept him awake while waiting.

Colorado weather was one of the reasons he'd been eager to leave Southern California. He had loved the cold and the snow ever since that first family ski trip when he was little. Every good memory he had was in the snow, and he was grateful Cassidy had broken up with him in the summer. It meant the winter still belonged to him.

He rubbed his eyes again beneath his sunglasses. The line at Carl's Café was taking forever. It had been this way all fall ever since Carl's daughter, Carly, had left for college. It meant the line was longer than usual, but people didn't seem to mind. Carl was so proud, telling anyone who would listen about her full-ride scholarship to Berkeley. Since Austin had friends there, the teen had asked him hundreds of questions before she left, which he'd been happy to answer.

Austin nodded in greeting to those who said hello to him. It was the usual early-morning crowd. There were parents with kids in strollers and teachers grabbing a cup of coffee to go on their way to school. Tina Page was eating breakfast with her wife before opening the bookshop down the street. He waved at Mrs. Foster, the sweet but sharp elderly woman who was often at Miller Family Medical for one reason or another. She looked to be in good form today as she waved, chatting away with a friend over pancakes.

After almost three years working in Jasper Creek, he was now as fixed a part of the town as they all were, even if he technically lived outside of it. The quiet predictability that had been a welcome escape after his breakup had become a stifling tedium that no number of puzzles could alleviate. He knew everyone in the café this morning, knew their names, where they worked, and if they were up to date on their vaccines.

Then he noticed a tall guy standing by the takeout counter, tapping his foot and scrolling his phone like he was late for something important.

He wasn't someone who lived in town, but he did look familiar. Austin's brain lit up, shaking itself out of its stupor like a sleepy cat who caught sight of a bird outside. Someone he recognized but didn't know the name. Who could it be?

The excitement was short-lived, unfortunately. The connection clicked a few seconds later when he saw Clementine Miller hovering behind him. It was her boss from the PT clinic, Marius something? Mike? Anais had told him at some point, but they hadn't started referring patients there until Clementine had joined that summer, first as an intern, then as a full-time PT. To have a big, new clinic come into town and not reach out directly to other doctors in the area had rubbed the staff at Miller Family Medical the wrong way.

Seeing him in person, Austin was even less of a fan. He'd grown up wealthy and was familiar with those who aspired to it, grasping at it with both hands and holding it tight once they had it. This guy was a textbook case in subtle ways only Austin would notice. The brand of his sneakers and style of winter coat. The casual yet posed way he leaned against the counter as he waited for his food. The impressive height of his pompadour, which must be hairsprayed better than a beauty queen's to stay in place in this kind of weather.

Austin placed his order with Carl and stepped into the small waiting crowd just behind Clementine. She hadn't noticed him yet since her eyes were still focused on the back of her boss's head. It was the familiar look of longing Austin remembered seeing on her face when he'd first started working at Miller Family Medical and Clementine had been their shy but quietly sassy receptionist. Being a smart woman, the crush she'd had on him back then had long since faded. She talked to him now like he was anybody else.

Or at least, she did when she wasn't absorbed in staring at someone else. Her shoulders rose with a deep breath before she took a tentative step forward, putting to use the courage Austin had watched her slowly build up over the past few years.

Shame she was using it to talk to someone Austin wouldn't have even given the time to.

"Hey, morning, uh, good morning, Mark." Pink swept across her cheeks and her hands were shaking at her sides.

When Mark looked up from his phone, a hand went to his hair to smooth it out in what was clearly a routine gesture. A muscle in Austin's cheek twitched as he tried to suppress an eye roll.

"Oh hi, Clem." There was the smallest tilt of his mouth, then his eyes slid back to his phone.

Clementine bit her lip and took a step back, defeat shining on her face and in her now moist eyes. A cold breeze blew in from the open door, sending a shiver down Austin's neck.

Austin didn't know why he did it. Maybe because he'd been so freaking bored lately and it had been ages since he'd provoked a poser like Mark. Maybe because she looked so hurt by the guy's dismissal of her when she clearly thought the world of him. Austin had been on the receiving end of a brush-off like that. The memory of the first time he passed Cassidy at the Centennial U Hospital after the breakup was three years old but still stung like it had happened a few minutes ago.

Or maybe he did it because after watching Clementine bloom over the past few years, he hated anyone who made her retreat again into the timid, uncertain shell of a person she used to be. Seeing her at the Fall Festival the week before with her family was the real Clementine: teasing, funny, loving, open. Sure, she was still a little intimidated by Anais, but that was normal with sisters. The timid mouse she was this morning with her joker of a boss was definitely not normal for Clementine, not anymore.

Confident Clementine was too interesting for him to ever want to see her disappear, even for a moment.

Whatever the reason, before he could come to his senses, he strode up to her, wrapped an arm around her shoulders, and planted a kiss on the top of her head.

"Is our food ready yet, sugar?"

The response was instantaneous, just as Austin knew it would be. The guy's eyes shot over to the two of them, took in Austin's arm around Clementine, and a storm cloud spread across his rugged features. Clearly Mark wasn't interested in Clementine, or he would have said hello properly, but he didn't want anyone else to be interested either. Fascinating.

Also, what a freaking jerk.

"Um, it's almost ready." To her credit, Clementine didn't pull away or react like this was anything unusual. She'd either be thrilled by his help or furious that he put her on the spot. From the tight tic of her jaw, Austin had a strong suspicion which one it was. "I think your oatmeal is taking longer than usual. I asked them to put some chia in it since I know you've been constipated lately."

A laugh burst out of Austin that he tried to turn into a cough. Oh, she was pissed all right. Good. He'd rather have her angry at him than afraid of some moron who didn't even say good morning to her.

"Thanks, angel. My colon appreciates it. Who's this?"

There was the slightest tremble in her body, then a tightening of all the muscles that were pressed against him. "Have you not met Mark Vickers yet?"

The guy's eyes hadn't left Austin's arm this entire time, but they finally moved up to his face, which Austin knew was looking fabulous, even exhausted and pre-caffeine. He squeezed Clementine even closer to his side, then stuck out his other hand.

"Hi, I'm Dr. Austin Gibson." Did he linger over the word *doctor*? Of course he did.

"Dr. Mark Vickers, DPT." He gave Austin a handshake that was a little too firm to be friendly. "Clem keeps talking about this place, so I thought I'd give it a try."

Adding an extra squeeze to the handshake, Austin kept his face neutral at the nickname he knew Clementine hated. If she hadn't said anything about it, she was crushing hard on this terrible guy. Who was also her boss.

Well, well, well. Wasn't Clementine Miller quite the puzzle?

"Order fifty-seven!" Carl called from behind the counter.

"That's me," Mark said, his eyes still on Austin's arm. "I hope it's as good as you say this place is, Clem."

"It's even better." Austin kept his gaze on the other man until he finally looked at him and nodded once.

"Well, she was right about the festival, so I trust her judgment."

Meaning he absolutely did not trust it when it came to Austin.

"Thanks, Mark." Beneath Austin's arm, Clementine had turned a bright pink and was looking at her boss with stars in her eyes. Had this guy never complimented her before? Or was she just thrilled to have him finally talking to her in complete sentences? "I hope you like the food."

"I'm sure I will." The smile Mark gave her was dazzling, the kind Austin saved for calling in major favors. It took a few deep breaths and physically biting his cheek for Austin to stop himself from punching Mark right then and there. "See you at the office in a little while."

There was the smallest nod at Austin, the bare minimum to be polite, and finally he was gone. Austin let out a breath, the tension leaving his shoulders as a grin spread across his face. He looked down at Clementine, and the grin disappeared.

Shining in her eyes was the familiar, dangerous glint he'd seen countless times in Anais's.

Austin was in serious trouble.

How delightful.

Clementine kept her lips turned up and eyes on the door until Mark had disappeared behind it.

Then she whirled around to face Austin.

"I can't believe you just did that," she whispered, blood boiling, pulse hammering in her ears, unsure if she wanted to hug him or throttle him.

"It worked though." His voice was soft and his eyes shone with mischief.

This caught her off guard. She narrowed her gaze. "What do you mean?"

"You wanted Matt's attention, right?"

"Mark."

He blinked his deep blue eyes slowly, the dark lashes fluttering. "Yeah, whatever. He wasn't even looking at you, but as soon as I came over, he looked like someone stole his donut."

Golden electricity shot through her chest. "Really?"

"Did you not notice?" Austin raised his perfect eyebrows.

"I was a little too focused on your arm wrapped around me." And the kiss on her forehead.

That half of Jasper Creek had seen.

The café was full of people eating their breakfasts, heads bent over their tables, but the excited murmur of new gossip was impossible to miss. The unexpected show of affection between the two of them had turned into a whisper fight. People might just explode from the secondhand drama.

"Come here." Clementine grabbed Austin's arm and dragged him outside, away from the curious eyes. Safe on the sidewalk with no one else around, she shoved her hands into her coat pockets and shivered. "You have no idea what you just did. Anais will know within the hour. My parents will hear about this. You have to tell them it was a joke."

He took his time wrapping his scarf around his neck, tying it in a complicated pattern that somehow made his eyes look even bluer.

"Or we don't." His ludicrous words were little white puffs in the chilly November morning. "We could pretend to date for a while."

The world tilted under her feet and warmth rushed to her head so fast she stumbled. With a strong, steady hand whose heat managed to penetrate the fabric of her thick winter coat, Austin kept her upright, his eyes never leaving hers.

The effort it took to breathe and form words deserved an Olympic medal. "I thought you were smart, but that's the stupidest thing I've ever heard."

His lips turned up, transforming his face into the devilish perfection she'd spent hours dreaming of back when they worked together. "I don't think Mike would like it much if we dated."

"Mark." The idea was too absurd to be true, but despite this morning's serious lapse in logical thought, Austin was the most intelligent person she knew. Not that she'd ever admit that to him.

She bit her lip. "What do you mean?"

"He clearly knows how you feel about him."

Dread dropped heavily into her stomach. "Wait, how do you know?"

Austin waved a hand, like it wasn't even worth his time to

answer that. Considering how she'd been staring at the back of Mark's head before Austin's little show, it had probably been obvious to anyone who'd been looking.

"In his mind, you're his."

"Excuse me?" The heat rose quickly in Clementine's face, and she turned in to the wind to let the cool air blast across her cheeks. There was no way that Mark saw her that way. No one had ever seen her that way. Not even Marbles was particularly interested in her. "Last time I checked, I was my own person."

"That's not what I meant, and you know it." Austin leaned against the building and crossed his arms. "Having a Miller on staff is doing wonders for his new business. He'd never risk messing anything up with you, but he figures he doesn't need to do much to keep you around, since you're so infatuated with him. Seeing you with someone else, however, would turn all that on its head. He's reconsidering your entire relationship now."

The patience in his voice wasn't belittling like it was when Anais explained something to her. He'd always been like that at the clinic, gentle with her, like he knew she wasn't quite as bulletproof as her sister but didn't think less of her for it.

"Seeing you with me will make it even worse. I'm much more attractive than he is."

Someone came out of the café and Austin nodded a greeting, and while Clementine moved to let them pass, she didn't look their way. She was too busy staring at Austin with her mouth open, wondering how he could suddenly be missing the mental sharpness she'd once been in awe of.

"I don't even know where to start with that. You're wrong about everything."

A single dark eyebrow lifted over eyes so blue they could be Pantone's color of the year. "So you don't think I'm more attractive than Martin?"

She sputtered. "That's not what I meant— You're both— It's

not the same—" Narrowing her eyes, she put her hands on her hips and approached him.

The sidewalk in front of the café was barely wide enough for one person, but he didn't budge from his relaxed stance against the building. She inhaled a shaky breath. After what he'd done in the café, it was hard to be this close to him and not want his arm around her again. Even if it had been just a show for Mark's benefit. "Fake dating is not something real people do. It's something you read about in books or see in cheesy movies on streaming services. It won't change anything about me and Mark."

"It will." The certainty in his voice made her want to throw something at him. "You were instantly more relaxed as soon as you were focused on me instead of him. That kind of confidence is very appealing."

She took a step back and rolled her eyes at his impossible cockiness, but her cheeks warmed from the idea of being appealing. To Mark or Austin or anyone, really. "I'm not his."

"Not in the way you want to be, but the attention from you feeds his ego."

"You'd know all about that, wouldn't you?"

He didn't respond, but a smug smile appeared on his face. Of course he knew how hot he was, how a single tilt of his lips could make women think and feel. Once you got past that, though, it was his intelligence and kindness that were truly breathtaking.

When he wasn't being a pompous know-it-all, that is.

She sighed and shook her head. The sun was peeking above the tree line, its pale warmth barely touching the top of the café. "Look, we're both late to work. Thanks for... whatever you did back there. But I don't need a repeat. Use that giant brain of yours to figure out how to explain this to Anais when she asks."

"She won't. It's too impossible for her to believe anyone who tells her about it."

The crush of disappointment hit Clementine hard enough to turn her breath into ice in her chest. Of course it was impossible.

Laughable really, that someone like Austin would ever be interested in her. Even Austin didn't think it was possible. Which didn't exactly support his theory that Mark would be jealous, since Mark was in that same gorgeous and smart stratosphere that could barely be seen from way down on earth.

"Goodbye, Austin." She turned on her heel and headed to her car without looking back.

At least he was smart enough not to follow her.

Vickers Physical Therapy was already buzzing by the time Clementine finally got there. Luckily, it didn't sound like anyone was talking about what had happened at the café.

Not yet anyway.

Clementine wasn't late for any appointments, but she liked to use the first hour of her morning to finish paperwork and go through her emails. She'd have to do that after work now. Which was fine. It wasn't like she had anyone to go home to see other than her cat, and Marbles had an automatic feeder.

There were five therapists working in the main treatment room that day, including Melissa who'd been at the Fall Festival, and she gave them all a nervous wave good morning. When nobody mentioned seeing her at the café with Austin, however, she relaxed. It turned out all the practicing she'd done in the car to explain what someone might have seen at Carl's wouldn't be needed. She inhaled slowly a few times, then fell into her regular rhythm of preparing for the day.

She opened up her computer on its rolling, standing desk, took a look at her busy schedule, then went to check she had all the equipment for her first appointment. Clearly what had happened with Austin wasn't as big a piece of Jasper Creek gossip as she'd thought. She should just forget about the whole thing, and his ridiculous suggestion they fake date.

The morning passed in the happy blur of treating patients she loved. When she'd worked at Miller Family Medical, people were only there when they felt awful, and you never got to see them get better. Here she was able to see the progress people made over the weeks she treated them. It was immensely satisfying.

Mostly, it was older patients, since that was Mark's specialty and Jasper Creek's population skewed older. But there was a smattering of young professionals, transplants from Denver looking for cheaper housing and the flexibility to work at home. Unfortunately, the toll their body took spending all day hunched over a computer typing, without the regular interruptions of walking around an office, was clear to see. There was only so much Clementine could do for them, but she showed them all the same exercises and hoped they'd remember to do them in between meetings. She wished she could pop up on their screens with tailormade routines or set calendar reminders for them to stretch.

By the time lunch rolled around, Clementine was starving. The appointments were staggered so she could eat alone, which she preferred. Though she loved interacting with patients and her colleagues were all great, she was an introvert at heart. She needed downtime during the day, or she got totally wiped out.

In a family of extroverts, this peace was hard to come by. It made her feel all that more separate from her siblings. She went out for their sake but would always prefer one-on-one time. It was part of why she'd decided to live on her own when she moved home, rather than move back in with her parents.

Though it would have meant better food. Her dad was a great cook, always had been, but that gene had skipped Clementine. She took a bite of her sad sandwich and frowned in the empty break room.

Of course Mark walked in at that exact moment.

"Everything okay, Clem?" He pulled a Tupperware container from the fridge and sat across from her, clueless that this simple act had sent her heart into overdrive.

"Um, yeah. Just not a great sandwich." The second the words were out of her mouth, she regretted them. Trying to keep her whole body from trembling, her hand fisted on her leg underneath the table.

This has never happened before. Not only did he usually eat lunch in his office, they'd never sat face-to-face like this since he'd interviewed her months ago for an internship. What was she supposed to do? To say? If her blood could quiet down in her ears, she might be able to think of something.

"I thought maybe something happened with your boyfriend." He tilted his head to the side. "How long have you been with Dr. Green?"

"Gibson." The panicked beat of her pulse in her eyes was making her dizzy, so she wasn't even sure she'd heard him correctly.

"Right. Him." Mark took a bite of what looked like pasta salad, then looked at her, eyebrows raised.

"Oh!" Surprise shook her out of her wordless stupor. He really was asking about Austin. And her. No one had mentioned Austin to her all morning, but maybe none of them had been at the café. She should have expected the one person she knew for sure had seen them to bring him up. Could she be fired for lying? "Um, not long."

Technically true.

"Hm." This noncommittal grunt was hard to understand. Clementine kept her hands in her lap, her ham and cheese sandwich abandoned. Not that her churning stomach could have kept anything down right now anyway. "How'd you meet?"

"He's a friend of my sister's." Also technically true. Her stomach dove toward the floor. "He works at Miller Family Medical with Anais and my dad. He started back when I was still a receptionist there, but we didn't get together until recently."

Very recently.

"Ah." Mark nodded and chewed for a moment. "How were your patients this morning?"

"Fine." The sudden switch in topic was confusing but a relief. Some of the tension left Clementine's stomach, and they fell into an easy conversation about treatment plans. He answered some of the questions she'd usually ask one of the more senior therapists.

It was the longest conversation they'd ever had, and Clementine was amazed at how she was able to talk without trouble. Much easier than it had been at the festival, when she'd babbled like a love-struck teenager.

Or a love-struck twenty-five-year-old, which was somehow worse. Shouldn't she know how to do this by now?

Today it felt like she did know, at least a little. The words flowed easily, and she found herself relaxing into the conversation. The clinic was big, and he wasn't here every day. He had so much to do as the owner of two different locations that they didn't have much regular interaction, which only made her crush more intense whenever she did see him.

This one-on-one lunch was as unexpected as it was perfect. This was exactly what she'd hoped for when she started her PT journey: learning from someone who was doing exactly what she wanted to do someday.

He even shared her frustration with the office worker patients who never seemed to be able to stick to a treatment plan.

"If you have any brilliant ideas to get them to actually do the exercises more than the once or twice a week they're in the clinic, I'd love to hear them." Mark shook his head and took another bite of his lunch.

The overhead light was harsh, highlighting lines to his face she'd never noticed before, giving him a weathered kind of rugged attractiveness. It reminded her of Austin, who had similar lines around his mouth when he smiled. Both men were unbearably attractive, but Austin was more familiar. That's all she needed, really, to get used to Mark. Today was a good start.

Maybe there was a way to keep it going?

"Actually, there is something I've been thinking about."

She didn't know why she said it, but when his eyes lit up and his mouth spread in a smile, the thump of her heart was all the encouragement she needed to keep going.

"What if we did little videos on social media?" When his smile slipped, she rushed on, needing to get it out before he could cut her off the way Anais had when she'd asked if it was something she'd ever considered for the family's medical practice. "It would make it easy for people to follow, since they're on their phones all day anyway. We could post at the same time every day so they know to check it at their lunch break or whenever. It would also be good advertising for the clinic. Get some new clients."

Mark pursed his lips and didn't say anything for a moment.

Well, clearly he hates that idea.

She crushed her napkin in her hand and stood up. "It was just a thought."

"It's not a bad one. Let's keep talking about it."

Clementine froze, halfway out of her seat. Was this really happening? A normal conversation with him that led to her not only sharing her idea but him liking it as well?

"Maybe tonight? If you're not busy with Austin, that is."

Her stomach sank.

Austin had been right. For whatever reason, dating him—or at least pretending to—had gotten Mark's attention. Even though she'd never admit it, it might have also helped her feel more at ease around Mark during their conversation and had given her the boost she needed to tell him about her video idea.

"I'm meeting him right after work."

Seeing Austin had been the last thing on her mind that morning when she left him in front of Carl's, but it was a sure thing now.

Mark's lips pursed in displeasure, and she bit back a groan.

She could practically see Austin's victorious smirk already.

FOUR

AUSTIN

"I saw you this morning at the café."

Mrs. Foster had been seated on the exam table for the past ten minutes while Austin went through some routine health questions. Clearly she'd been saving this little pronouncement for the right moment, trying to catch him off guard.

He slipped on his most charming smile, the one he knew could distract even the most fervent busybody. Clementine had been clear that she didn't want to go along with his plan—the one he was certain would get her the results she desired—so he had to make sure his impromptu display of affection wouldn't make her life more difficult. "I saw you too. I believe I waved hello, so I hope you're not trying to tell me I ignored you."

The seventy-seven-year-old gave him a stare that spoke to the decades of gossip she'd personally shepherded through Jasper Creek. "You're a smart man, Dr. Gibson. You know that's not what I'm talking about."

So far, amazingly, she'd been the only one to say anything. Anais somehow wasn't aware, and none of the other patients he'd had all day had mentioned anything. Perhaps not as many people as he anticipated had noticed them together.

Or, just like he'd reassured himself several times throughout the day, they saw it and assumed it was friendly. Clementine was, after all, a Miller, and Austin had been working with Anais and her father for a few years. It would be within the range of normal to greet Clementine with a hug. And the forehead kiss had been small, meant only for Mark to see.

Mark, the complete idiot who wouldn't even acknowledge an employee when she was right behind him. What kind of boss was he? Austin had had many over the years, and they ranged from completely hands off to wanting to be best friends with everyone. Dr. Miller fell somewhere in between, happy to help and advise when asked, but he trusted his staff to do what was needed.

Thanks to his association with the Millers, the town had adopted Austin as one of their own, which was another reason he kept his dating pool firmly outside town limits. That didn't stop rumors from swirling anytime he gave someone a second look, and now Mrs. Foster had caught a glimpse of something even better.

"If there were anything to know, you'd already know it." Austin held up the blood pressure cuff. "Please roll up the sleeve of that lovely sweater for me."

"Hm." The older woman's lips pursed, and she obediently held out her arm. Austin knew she had more to say, but he was nothing if not adept at directing attention to the patient, where it belonged.

Once their appointment was over and he walked Mrs. Foster out into the empty waiting room, he was technically done for the day. Hunter at the front desk had already left, and Dr. Miller was still in his office, where he'd stay for another hour, then close up and return home to cook for his wife, who was head of radiology at Centennial University Hospital.

It was a routine that Austin might have had for himself, if things with Cassidy had gone differently. He leaned against the reception desk and stared out the window at the lamplit street in front of the office, the conversation with Mrs. Foster still running through his mind. He was certain he'd done enough to quell her curiosity, but there was no getting away from the fact that his life was inextricably tangled with the Millers. Which, a few years ago, had been exactly what he'd wanted. Now, however, he wasn't so sure.

From down the hall, Austin could hear Dr. Miller on the phone with his wife, asking her what she wanted for dinner. Austin had worked with Dr. Heather Miller during his time at CUH, but he'd left before his fellowship in emergency medicine had finished to come work in Jasper Creek. While he could easily get updates on what was happening at the hospital, he preferred knowing as little as possible about what his ex was up to.

The reminder of Cassidy was constant, however. As long as he worked with the Millers, as long as he knew he could get all the information he wanted with just a quick chat with Heather, he knew he'd never truly be free of that past. Just like with his patients, clean breaks were always best. Leaving California for good was what it had taken to find the balance he needed with his family. If he had any openings, any possibilities to easily fall back into old patterns, he'd do it. Especially when he was as bored as he was right now.

It wasn't the first time he'd thought about leaving Jasper Creek, but like every other time the idea popped into his head, he let it pass through him without latching on too hard. There were too many positives to truly consider it. Working with Anais, even as crabby as she was right now, was great. Gabby was out on maternity leave, but once she was back, it would be even better. As dull as things were for the moment, it wouldn't last.

Especially once Clementine realized he'd been right.

With a sigh that was more ennui than exhaustion, Austin turned off the lights in the waiting room. As he moved toward the front door to lock it, he saw Clementine walking up the steps, her expression scrunched into a familiar, furious thundercloud. A grin spread across his face.

Right on time.

Heart pattering eagerly, he couldn't keep the triumphant tone out of his voice when he opened the door for her.

"You look like you have something to say." The possibilities were few, but he had a hunch which was right. And his hunches were almost always true, in life and in medicine. "Is it 'you were right, Austin?' because I always love hearing that."

"I'm sure you do." As she stormed past him into the clinic, Clementine shot him a look that was eerily like the one her sister Anais gave him whenever he was being particularly obnoxious. "You'll never hear me say that, however."

Austin's grin widened to its full wattage, and Clementine blinked a few times, like she'd been temporarily blinded.

That had never happened with Anais. It had stopped happening with Clementine, too, after she'd started PT school. There was an unexpected rumble of pleasure in his chest to know that even if her heart belonged to the moron Mark, she wasn't fully immune to "the Austin effect" as Gabby liked to call it.

"So what are you here to say?" He leaned against the closed door and crossed his arms.

"Is my dad here?" She looked past the reception area shrouded in shadows to the hallway that was still lit.

"He's in his office."

She walked down the hall without looking back at him, and his interest was piqued in a way it hadn't been in months. Normally, he always knew what people would do. He could read a room, read someone's intentions. It was a game he'd played since he was young, a way to hone the observational skills that made him such a good doctor.

So far Clementine had been almost as predictable as her sister. Even if Anais hadn't fully seen it yet, Austin had known in his gut what a positive impact on her confidence there'd be when Clementine went to PT school in Colorado Springs rather than close by in Denver. Spending time on her own, away from the large Miller clan, had been the best thing she could have done—it was clear as day to Austin. As clear as the fact she was here tonight because he'd been right about Mark's reaction to seeing Austin with her.

But this sudden change in direction toward her father stirred a prickle of interest. Of fun.

He followed her down the hall and watched her knock on the door to Dr. Miller's office.

"Dad?"

"Minnie!" Austin could hear the joy in the older physician's voice. "Well, this is a nice surprise."

"I finished up early with my patients and saw the light was still on. Why don't you go home early? I can tidy up for you."

The staff was supposed to all take turns closing up the clinic every night, doing the simple things like making sure there were no dirty dishes in the break room or stray magazines floating around the reception area. Hunter did a good job before he left, but there were always little things people forgot.

"Oh, I can't ask you to do that." Dr. Miller's tone was firm, but a thread of tiredness leaked through.

"Austin's here. He'll help me." The smile on her face disappeared when she turned back to raise an eyebrow at him as if to threaten, *you'd better stay*.

The grin on his face was so wide now, his cheeks hurt. Oh, she was definitely way more fun than he'd been expecting. Of course, she was here to agree to his fake dating idea, but that didn't mean she was going to make it easy on him.

Good.

He had no idea what had happened to make her agree, and the mystery was more entertaining and exciting than anything that had happened lately.

"Well, if you're sure..." There was the distinct sound of shuffling papers. Unable to deny his kids anything if they requested outright, Dr. Miller was packing up for the night. "Thank you, Minnie."

Austin didn't move from his position against the wall until the older doctor came out into the hallway. Clementine was being very careful not to look at Austin, keeping her eyes on her father while a slow creep of red made its way up her neck.

He pushed off the wall to shake Dr. Miller's hand in parting. The second he was out the door, Austin walked into the break room, knowing Clementine would be right behind him. She stomped into the room and immediately began wiping down the counter, just like she'd done back when she'd been the receptionist.

"Has no one done this since I left?" she muttered.

Fighting the urge to laugh, he grabbed the broom in the corner. "Did you consider I might have plans tonight that don't involve tidying up the clinic?"

She whirled, worry etched on her face in stark lines that made her dark eyes shine. "Do you? I'm sorry. Go, we can do this later."

Hmm, that wasn't quite the courageous Clementine he'd come to expect recently. He stopped sweeping and waved a hand. "Don't worry. I don't have plans. I was just teasing."

In an instant, that fierce look was back on her face. "So then why aren't you helping?"

A short burst of a laugh escaped him before he bent to whisk everything at his feet into the dustbin. Austin forgot sometimes that though she had four siblings, just like he did, teasing was a form of love language for the Millers in a way it wasn't for the Gibsons.

Clementine left him to finish sweeping and walked out into the hall, presumably to check the reception area for any stray magazines or forms.

No, she definitely wasn't going to make this easy on him.

Excellent.

FIVE

AUSTIN

Austin took his time sweeping the break room, getting into all the nooks and crannies. If she was going to make things challenging, then he'd do the same. She could wait a few more minutes to tell him he was right.

When he finally joined Clementine, she was sitting behind the reception desk in the swiveling chair. It was a familiar sight that tugged at something deep in Austin's chest. The first six months of his time in Jasper Creek, he'd walked in to see the same thing every morning. Those early days after moving away from Denver, away from his job at CUH, were still some of the hardest. He'd been grateful for the fresh start Anais had provided him, and the change of pace had been just what he needed. The work of a small-town physician was much more satisfying for him than the endless bureaucracy and politics of the hospital. At least it had been at first.

Waking up alone every day, going home to an empty house every night, as comforting as it had been initially, wasn't the life he wanted for himself forever. Everything was about balance. If things were stressful at work and at home, like they had been those last few months at CUH, then life was wretched, just like he'd been. But the opposite was true as well. It could be quiet at work or quiet at home, but not both, or he'd fall into the languid restlessness he'd been plagued with for months.

"Are you okay?" Frowning, Clementine tilted her head as she took in Austin's pensive expression.

"Fine." He ran a hand through his hair, mussing it in the very particular way he knew made his eyes stand out even more. "Just thinking."

"When are you ever not?"

He chuckled at that, then leaned on the high desk that separated the receptionist's area from the waiting room. She swirled back and forth in the chair just like she used to.

"I did like working here, you know." She bit her lip. "With you."

"Did you?" He raised an eyebrow as his heart gave an unexpected thump. "I don't remember us speaking all that much." She'd been quiet with him, but watching her with her sister and father, it had been easy to spot the flickers of savvy sassiness that he was now getting in full force.

"Yes, well... you can be quite intimidating when you want to be." She rolled her eyes. "As I'm sure you're well aware."

He grinned. He was very aware. "So why are you more comfortable with me now?"

"I don't know." The tips of her ears turned pink. She swiveled away from him in the chair, and he leaned forward over the desk to be sure he'd catch her eye when she finally turned back to face him.

"Yes you do."

"You want me to say it?" Her back was to him, but she peeked over her shoulder.

He nodded. "If you're really considering my plan of pretending to date me to get your boss to pay more attention to you, then you'll need to be honest with me." Honesty was something he'd assumed he had with Cassidy, until she'd proven just how ignorant he could be about some people.

Her foot tapped against the floor. She twisted the chair to the side, keeping her cautious gaze on him. "Who said I'm considering it?"

He sighed, then spread his hands on the desk, wiping away dust that only he could see. She was making this more difficult than it had to be for both of them. "Why else would you be here, *Clem*?"

Her shoulders tightened all the way up to her ears. She was getting close, but wasn't quite there yet. "I hate that nickname."

"I know." He smiled, the smug little one he knew would irk her. That irritation would smooth away her lingering anxiety at finally saying out loud what she needed to admit to him if they were going to succeed at this fake dating plan.

It took a minute longer than he expected, but the smile worked. She leaned back in the chair and let out a groan. "I'm comfortable around you now because I have a massive crush on my boss, and my brain only has space to be an anxious mess around one guy at a time."

Even though he knew that's what she was going to say, there was a strange cramp in his chest to hear her so adamant in her feelings for Mark. It wasn't jealousy, not really. Despondency maybe? After all, Clementine had gotten to know him better over the years and yet preferred someone as idiotic as Mark Vickers. Whenever someone got to really know Austin, that's always what happened.

"And?" He tapped a finger on the desk, waiting for the rest of it. It was like pulling teeth, and he'd never wanted to be a dentist.

Bringing her hands to cover her face, she did a full circle in the chair before saying more. "And he talked more to me today than he has since I started working there this summer, so your ridiculous demonstration this morning clearly worked, and we should keep doing it."

The despondency passed in a flash, and his lips curled in delicious mocking. Now they were getting somewhere. "Keep doing what?"

"Keep pretending to date."

"You assume my offer is still on the table." He stepped away from the desk and turned up his chin.

"Austin, you wouldn't have made me sit here and spill my secrets if you weren't planning on helping me." She crossed her arms and gave him a sardonic glare that he'd never seen on any of her siblings. This look was all Clementine. "You're astute, not an asshole."

The smile froze on his face. It was probably the first time anyone had summarized him so perfectly with so few words. It was easier when people thought he was an asshole.

He quickly recovered. If he was going to be bested by one of the Millers, it made sense that it would be her. She said the least, observed the most, and was brave enough on top of all that to step out of the path they'd laid out for her. Ruining all the plans Anais had for Miller Family Medical couldn't have been easy for Clementine to do, and Austin was still in awe two years later that she'd gone through with it. It reminded him of his own split with what people had expected of him, given who his family was.

"Of course I'll help you. I just had to make you squirm a little first." He came around to the other side of the desk and leaned on the wall, directly in front her. In response, she sat up a little straighter in her chair. Excellent. She'd need some backbone for this next part of the discussion. "Should we move on to rules around kissing in public?"

She sank into the chair, and the pink tinge was back in her ears. He'd seen it happen before. The blush on her neck would creep up while the one in her ears would trickle down, and they'd join in the middle of her cheeks. They weren't quite there yet, so he knew he could push her a little more.

"Or you could tell me what's in it for you," she said. Her body stilled, she threw her shoulders back, and her gaze turned steely.

Perfect, she was pushing back. This would be no fun otherwise.

"I like helping the Millers." He picked up the stapler from the desk and moved it to the other side of the keyboard.

She put the stapler back where it had been, eyes never leaving his. "Nope, not good enough."

"I'm bored." This, at least, was closer to the truth. He ran a hand through his hair. "Gabby's out on maternity leave for another month, and Anais will be soon. Both of them have been no fun at all since getting married. All happy and joyful."

"Yes, they are quite irritating..." Clementine's eyes took on a mischievous glint. "We could be even more obnoxious. More dopey."

"I like where your mind is headed."

She scooted back in the chair, putting some space between them so she could look him up and down. Slowly, like she was processing everything he said, weighing it for the same honesty he'd asked from her. "But it's still not good enough. We'd have to date at least through the New Year for it to be believable, and you're not giving up almost three months of your dating life just to annoy Anais."

"Maybe I need a break from my dating life."

Uh oh, this was very close to the truth. How had that slipped out? She was better at this than he'd expected. A shivery anticipation ran through his chest.

"You just said you were bored, so I know you're looking for fun, just not the kind you're used to. But that's still not all you want."

"Has anyone told you that you're irritatingly observant?" He tried to push at her chair with his foot, get her to spin around again, but she planted her feet and refused to give way.

"Come on, Austin, there has to be something you want."

He hesitated, then gave a dramatic shrug like this was the only thing he could think of. Like he hadn't been thinking about his sister's text all day. Like the trip wasn't on his mind the entire year.

"My family has this annual ski trip at Mammoth Mountain. If you want, you could come with me. It would get them to stop badgering me about still being single."

She tilted her head, her hair falling in waves over her shoulder. Unlike her sisters with their raven black locks, her hair was a medium brown that shone different colors depending on the light. It was like Clementine in that way. Unpredictable, changing depending on the situation. Right now, in the dim light of the empty office, the only light coming from a streetlamp outside, her hair was a deep chestnut, almost black. The black of a midnight lake on a hot summer night, inviting you to dive deep and cool your burning skin.

"I'll go with you, Austin." Her voice was soft, her eyes understanding. His heart thumped against his rib cage, eager yet tender. Then her gaze shifted to the desk in front of her. "But I can't ski."

Interesting. That wasn't what he'd expected her to say. "How do you not know how to ski? The mountains are right there. Everyone in Jasper Creek goes skiing."

She shrugged. "It was never my thing."

There was something there, something deeper, but Austin was already shaken enough. No sense drowning himself before they'd even gotten started.

"I can teach you."

"In a month? I doubt it."

The second the words left her mouth, she gasped and shot back a foot in her chair, bumping into the wall opposite the desk. Austin grinned widely. She knew she'd made a mistake.

"Is that a challenge?"

She buried her face in her hands. "I guess that'll give us at least a few plausible dates."

"We should probably begin with something more local. An evening at the Floodline will be enough to get started."

"We agree up front how many dates this will involve. Define

parameters around other things." Her bottom lip disappeared under her front teeth. "Physical interactions, for example."

The words "define parameters" had short-circuited his brain, so he almost missed the second part of what she'd said. Physical interactions with Clementine weren't something he'd ever thought about, but now that she'd said it, it was like the idea had always been there, waiting patiently to be spotted.

The hug in the café had felt so natural, the forehead kiss like something he'd done a thousand times already. It had been the most unthinking thing he'd done in ages, and just imagining doing it again was sending waves of complicated emotions through his chest.

This was his friend's sister. His boss's daughter. Someone he'd known for three years and had worked with for part of that. He'd been to her parents' house for parties and had gone out for drinks with her brother and brother-in-law.

The last thing he should be thinking about was any kind of physical interaction with her.

It would probably be a lot of fun.

Austin cleared his throat. "If you want to keep this going through the New Year, we should at least see each other weekly. Maybe twice a week."

When her eyes widened, he kept going. "It'll give you something to talk about at work."

She was still furiously biting her lip. Austin had to make a fist to stop himself from reaching out to tug gently at it while he waited for her reply. Finally, she nodded. "Two dates per week gives us stories to tell your family too."

"Right." Because that's what he was getting out of this. An escape from the annoyingly attentive glances of his sisters, his brother, and his parents. They were all so concerned, too concerned, that he hadn't been with anyone since Cassidy. Like his life wasn't complete without someone. Like whatever unforgivable wrong she'd done to him could only be fixed by a new girlfriend.

If the emptiness of his hookups over the past few years were any indication, they were probably right.

Austin hated it when someone else was right.

"Physical interactions don't have to be anything you don't want." Why was his voice suddenly rough and scratchy? He cleared his throat. "We can limit it to holding hands or an arm around the shoulder. Kissing on hands or hair only, never the face."

Something that might have been disappointment flickered across her features. "That sounds... fine." There was a tug deep in his gut.

Clementine stood suddenly and took out her phone. "Come here, we should take a picture."

"Of what?"

"My lock screen should be a picture of us." She narrowed her eyes and scanned him. "Or just you."

Without warning, she snapped a photo of him exactly as he was, leaning against the wall, halfway distracted and exhausted from his workday.

A smile spread across his face.

"Oh, that's perfect." She shifted her position and took a few more.

"You're quite the devious one, aren't you? I didn't even think about lock screens."

"You're never on your phone, that's why. It's much more important for my generation."

The laugh that burst out of him released some of the tension that he had kept in while thinking about his family's reaction to the news he'd be bringing someone this year.

"I'm only a year older than Bastien and Anais."

"Who are in their thirties." She wrinkled her midtwenties nose at him. "You were born in an entirely different decade."

He shook his head, happy to see her teasing instead of tense.

"Should we take a few pictures together, or will I just look like a dinosaur next to you?"

She tilted her head, scanning him with narrowed eyes. "I think you'll do."

Another laugh rippled through him, and he got a smirk in response from Clementine.

If fun was what he was looking for, then this might just be the best idea he'd ever had.

SIX

CLEMENTINE

This was the worst idea she'd ever had. Clementine stumbled and tried to get her muscles to cooperate, but they all turned to rubber the second Austin's hand appeared at her lower back, guiding her into the Floodline. The stares that met her as they walked into the bar were like little pinpricks all over her skin, tiny knives cutting into her, making her bleed out in public.

She hated blood. That's why she was a PT and not a physician like the rest of her family.

"Relax." Austin's voice was soft in her ear, the pressure of his hand a warm reminder she wasn't alone. "People will think you're mad at me."

This made her snort-laugh, and her stomach unclenched as Austin slipped his hand off her back and into hers. The dozens of eyes were still boring holes into her, but the blood was now pooling in her cheeks, so at least it was staying in her body.

"I am mad at you." She slid her eyes to his, if only to avoid looking at everyone whose necks were craning as they walked toward a booth, now hand in hand.

The corners of his lips turned up, but he kept his focus ahead. "Oh?"

"Yes. We had a big fight about where to go tonight, and you won."

"I highly doubt that. You are very convincing when you want to be."

They were at the booth now, and he let go of her hand only long enough to slide into his seat. Then he reached across and took both of her hands on top of the table, gazing into her eyes in what could only be described as adoringly.

If the heat sinking down her face and into her neck was any indication, her entire body was red now. No one had ever looked at her like that.

It's all pretend.

Like she'd been dunked into the creek in winter, Clementine cooled off.

"I don't think anyone could outsmart you." She tugged at her hands, but he held on tight.

"You'd be surprised how stupid I get when I'm in love."

A sharp inhale and her gaze locked on his.

Just pretend.

The longer she looked, however, the more she noticed the truth in his words. Something in the corner of his eyes, something sad and vulnerable.

Damn if it didn't make him that much more attractive. Like he needed the help.

"So what stupid things will you be doing with me?"

"That all depends." He laced his fingers in hers, tracing her palms, the touch of his fingers on her skin sending shivers up and down her spine. She closed her eyes and let herself believe, just for a moment, this was real, and someone was so obsessed with her that they couldn't stop touching her, looking at her, thinking about her.

Clementine sighed and opened her eyes. "Depends on what?"

"If Marius shows up."

"Mark."

"Whatever. I'm not the one with a crush on him." His lips were curled up.

Right, this was all to get Mark's attention. Which she definitely had gotten that afternoon at work when he asked if she had any plans that weekend. It was the first time he'd ever asked her that, just her, not a general question to the entire staff.

It had given her more than a little satisfaction to see his eyes darken when she said, in what she hoped was a casual, nonchalant way, "I'm meeting my boyfriend at the Floodline later."

Just as Austin had predicted when he'd suggested it, Mark had managed to invite himself. "I've never been, but it looks like a cool place. Maybe I'll see you guys there?"

And now, a few hours later, it was all Clementine could do not to look at the door every few seconds. Gazing at Austin dreamily like they were on a date was what she should be doing, and it wasn't that hard to convince her eyes to stare at him. Especially when he was still stroking her hands like they were precious objects.

"It's not a hard name. Neither is yours. I don't know why neither of you can seem to remember."

Austin's eyebrow popped up. "He messed up my name? This is already having the intended impact then."

"Does that mean more dates are needed, or less?"

"We're not even halfway through the first, and you're already ready to dump me?" He shook his head, a laugh trembling at the edges of his mouth. "At least wait until tomorrow morning like most women."

Instead of reassuring Clementine, this sparked a tug of nerves deep in her chest. "Austin, do I need to be worried about running into any of your exes here?"

She hadn't thought about it earlier since her own dating history was nonexistent. There was no need to give Austin the heads-up about anyone. Though Clementine couldn't remember hearing anything about him dating someone in Jasper Creek, there had been chatter since the moment he arrived in town about the string of women he'd been with. Not that she'd paid that much attention, and she'd been away at school the past few years.

The truth could be very different from what little she knew about his past. The last thing their first fake date needed was an awkward encounter in the Floodline to turn her nerves into pure humiliation.

"I only have one significant ex, and she's in Denver. I don't think she even knows or cares where I live now."

Her heart twisted at his words. This was more information than she'd been expecting, more of that endearing vulnerability she'd gotten a few tantalizing hints of. But it wasn't quite what she'd meant.

"I meant like... ex-flings or whatever." She shifted, now tugging harder at him to release her hands, but he held even tighter than before.

"Flings?" He let out a soft chuckle. "I'll answer your question if you say the word."

She squirmed even more now, writhing in her seat in embarrassment. Why was Austin doing this to her? His expression hadn't changed. He still had that adoring look on his face. He was the master of making her uncomfortable, and she wanted to prove to him that he didn't affect her like that. Putting him in his place was fun, and she wasn't about to lose this battle, no matter how much he tortured her.

Taking a breath, she steeled her spine and looked him straight in the eye. "Any jealous former lovers I should be worried about interrupting our night?"

Now the smile that spread across his face could almost be described as proud. His eyes alighted with mischief. He put both of her hands in his and brought them to his lips to plant a kiss on them, his eyes never leaving hers. "Nope. Nothing to worry about."

The warmth of his kiss on her hands made its way up her arms and through her body.

It's all pretend.

"Well, good. I'd hate for them to interrupt such a beautiful performance."

A laugh rumbled through him before his eyes flicked over her shoulder and his expression shifted.

"Oh, I'm just getting started. Can I get you something from the bar?"

"A pint of chocolate peanut butter please." While the Floodline had excellent beer, it was their ice cream that would soothe her anxiety right now.

He nodded, then slid out of the booth, her hands finally free from his grasp. The lack of him should have been a relief, but instead, she felt empty. It was nice to be sitting here with someone, holding hands. It was nice to not be alone.

While he made his way up to the bar, she cast a quick glance over her shoulder. Mark was standing by the door, holding it open for an older couple walking in. He gave them a brief, heartwarming smile, his eyes crinkling with kindness before scanning the crowd. She was tempted to wave, but would a girlfriend on a date do that? Probably not.

When his eyes landed on her, however, and he waved, she did the polite thing and gave a slight shake of her hand in his direction. He ambled over, his dark eyes still scanning the room. When they locked on something, she followed his gaze to Austin at the bar where he was chatting with Matt and Carter Hayes. The cousins were friends with the Millers, though Carter and his sister Isabelle were closer to Bastien and Anais, while Matt was younger than Clementine and had been in school with Dani.

Even with their family friends, there'd been no one just for Clementine. Everyone was either a few years older or younger. No one had been her friend first.

Austin definitely wasn't. He'd known Anais since residency,

would never have even talked to someone like Clementine if they hadn't worked together or if she wasn't the sister of someone he knew.

If this ridiculous plan worked, Mark would be hers in a way no one else was. Nobody in her family knew him, he was new to the area, and if she could trust Austin's judgment—which she did implicitly but would never admit to him—he already saw Clementine as his.

Not in the gross, women-as-property way. But she must already be someone special to him, or he wouldn't have shown up tonight. Fake dating Austin was already having some kind of impact. There was no doubt about it.

A jitter ran through her as Mark approached her table and smiled. "Hey, Clem. This is a cute place." He leaned forward and rested a hand on the back of the booth by her head.

She inhaled, then coughed when his strong cologne hit her nose. Cute wasn't quite how she'd describe the Floodline. "It used to be really rustic—log cabin vibes and moose heads on the wall. When the older Hayes siblings took it over, they did a gut renovation and now it's more industrial chic."

His lips ticked up, and he tapped his fingers against the worn leather of the booth. "You don't sound like you like that."

"It's fine." She took a tiny breath but got a mouthful of his cologne and held back a gag. He never wore it at the clinic, so this must be what he wore when he went out. It was the kind of information she was always hungry for about Mark, but it didn't give her the happy thrill she'd expected it to. Maybe because she was trying so hard not to breathe through her nose. "It just looks like every other bar now."

"That's not necessarily a bad thing."

Beneath the table, her hands squeezed into fists.

"It is when the bar is so different and you can't tell anymore just by looking at it. If something's special, you should be able to see it without someone telling you."

Maybe that was the key to getting where she wanted to be with Mark. He still saw her as just another employee. It wasn't like she carried around a sign listing everything she'd done to stand out, to make herself different from her family. Because she wasn't really that different, not in the ways that she wanted to be. Not yet anyway.

"What makes it so special?"

His eyes met hers and she inhaled sharply. Was he asking about her or about the bar? Just like at the Halloween Festival, too many things ran through her mind to be able to think of one.

"That would be the ice cream." Austin appeared behind Mark. They exchanged head nods in greeting, but there was a tension in their eyes that sent a shiver of eager anticipation through Clementine. "Here's your pint, Cutie."

"Cutie?" Mark's mouth turned down in a grimace, and he stepped back from the booth, the pungent musk clinging to his body finally disappearing from Clementine's immediate breathing space.

It wasn't the best nickname she'd ever had, but at least it was better than Clem. But only barely.

"Thanks, Dino." As in dinosaur. She smirked at Austin's scowl as he handed her the ice cream.

Mark shifted on his feet. "Well, I won't interrupt your date—"

"Please, join us." Austin slipped into the booth on the side next to Clementine, rather than across. He threw his arm over his shoulder. "Clementine never talks about you, so I'd love to learn more about the guy she works for."

Mark looked uncertain, his eyes dancing over the crowd as if searching for some reason, any reason, not to sit down. "Let me just grab a drink. Anything you recommend?"

Clementine opened her mouth to answer, but Austin spoke first, going on about the local IPAs and wheat beers the Floodline served, how they paired with the ice cream they made on the premises using milk from a local dairy. It should have been annoying, this show-off, smarty-pants routine. Anais and Gabby liked to tease him about it, but knowing it was for her benefit somehow made it less irritating. It was sweet, almost.

She snuggled back into the booth and lifted a hand to touch his arm that was wrapped around her. He gave her shoulder a gentle squeeze.

Pretend, pretend, pretend.

Given the glower on Mark's face, he definitely found Austin's long monologue annoying. Or maybe it was the way he was touching her? When Austin finally finished his spiel, Mark asked Clementine if he could get her anything, and she blurted out the first thing she could think of. Looking relieved, he wandered off in the direction of the bar.

Trying to scoot out of Austin's embrace, Clementine turned and glared at him. "Cutie? Really?"

But he just pulled her tighter to his side and leaned his head down close to her ear. The warmth of his breath caressed the side of her cheek, and she shivered, despite the heat of the bar.

"It's what clementines are called, aren't they?"

"Oh." That was kind of adorable, actually. "I thought you were patronizing me."

"Me? Never." His lips quirked up. "I do have some thoughts about Dino, however..."

A giggle escaped her, and she could feel the rumble of a laugh in his chest where it lay pressed against her side. "Shh, he's coming back."

"What was that? You'll have to speak up. My old ears can't hear you."

Now she was full on snickering by the time Mark sat down with the drinks. He raised an eyebrow as he held out Clementine's glass.

"I don't think I've ever heard you laugh." Mark took a sip of his beer, then his eyebrows shot up and he nodded once, like he approved. "This is good."

"You sound surprised," Austin said, an edge to his voice Clementine had never heard before.

"It's such a small place that I didn't think their beer would be on par with what you find in Denver."

"I meant about her laughing. Is physical therapy not a fun place to work?"

"The 'her' you're referring to is sitting right next to you." Clementine shifted under the weight of his arm on her shoulder and turned her head so he could see her glare. "And *she* has a lot of fun at work."

Now she turned back to Mark and gave him a smile. "I just usually have older patients, and they need a gentler touch. Not a stand-up comedy act."

The corners of Mark's lips turned up, and Clementine felt a rush of pride at his approval that was quickly washed away by the pressure of Austin's body against her side.

"If you're referring to the time I put on a clown nose and danced in the reception area, that was because Billy Taylor had strep and I was trying to make him feel better." Austin slid his arm off her shoulder and crossed his arms. The look of exaggerated indignation on his face was so ridiculous Clementine let out a snort-laugh.

"I've definitely never heard you make that sound." Mark chuckled.

In a cold flash of horror, the humor left her body. It was the least attractive sound ever, and she seemed to be making it quite a lot around Austin. Who wouldn't care, since he wasn't really dating her, but what if bothered Mark?

Pushing not so gently on her fake boyfriend's shoulder, she turned away from her boss's smirking face. "Let me out please. I need the restroom."

Maybe Austin could hear the embarrassment in her voice, or maybe he was just polite, but whatever the reason, she was grateful that he slid out of the booth without complaint.

Resisting the urge to look back, she made her way through the Friday night crowd to the bathrooms in the back of the bar and let the feeling of yet another failure with Mark wash over her.

As Austin watched Clementine run away from the booth like it was on fire, he bit back the rage creeping up his throat. She had to push her way through the half-drunk patrons, most of whom knew her and would be wondering what was happening. Some even tried to talk to her, probably asking what she was doing here with Austin.

He had one job tonight. Make sure Clementine had a good time so she could relax if Mark showed up. He'd failed. Not because of anything he'd done, but because the dummy sitting across from him was completely clueless about the effect his words had on her. The two men scowled at each other for a few minutes after Clementine left the table, waiting to see who'd break the tense silence first.

Finally, Austin crossed his arms, careful to keep his tone light. "She only laughs like that around me."

"I didn't realize you were such a funny guy." Mark took a sip of his beer and raised his eyebrows. "It's not what I hear about you."

"Oh yeah? And what do you hear exactly? That I'm everyone's favorite doctor?" He leaned back and draped his arms over the back of the booth.

"Not exactly." The other man's glare would have been dark and intimidating if Austin hadn't predicted this exact conversation.

It didn't matter who it was, how old they were, what they did for work. Every guy in Jasper Creek had the same reaction to Austin when they realized who he was and the reputation he had. It was as inevitable as it was banal. Sure, he'd kind of done it to himself. It would take less than a minute to find someone at the Floodline who could tell stories about all the women Austin had picked up at the bar over the years. Mark had probably overheard someone talking about him when he'd gone to get drinks.

This reaction was more than that, however. There was a personal edge to the resentment in his voice. A flicker of interest flared in Austin's chest. He racked his brain, trying to remember if he'd met Mark in Denver or even California, but there was no logical way he could have, and Austin had a prodigious memory for names and faces.

Before Austin could say anything else, however, Clementine was back at the table. Digging into the mystery of what Mark seemed to know about him would have to wait until the next time they met, which they were guaranteed to do, thanks to his deal with Clementine.

As she slid into the booth next to Austin, Mark stood up. "I've got to get going." He drained the last of his beer and set the glass on the table. "I'm meeting friends for dinner."

"It was nice seeing you tonight." Clementine's voice was too eager, too happy.

It was too obvious what she thought of Mark, but for whatever reason, the guy didn't seem to care. Mark only cared that she was with Austin and he didn't think she should be.

"Thanks for recommending this place. I'll definitely be back." With a nod at Austin that was barely a tilt of his chin, he grabbed his coat and headed out.

Next to him, Clementine sank back into the cushions and let out a breath. "Well, that was a disaster."

"Hardly." He looped his arm over her shoulder and pulled her close. The tickle of her hair against his cheek brought a smile to his lips. She'd left it loose tonight, the dark rainbow of browns sparkling in the lights of the bar. The urge to run his hands through it was easy enough to ignore, though he'd ask her later if they could include that in the physical interactions clause of their agreement. To make all this more convincing, of course, not because he was dying of curiosity to know what it felt like. "He absolutely hates me."

"And this is a good thing?"

"The more he hates me, the more he won't want you to be with me."

"That's not the same thing as wanting me."

Smart girl. That's exactly what he'd been trying to tell her without saying it.

"We can stop this right now if you want."

She shifted, drawing closer to him in the booth, and his heart beat against his rib cage. "I thought I should at least wait until tomorrow morning?"

He'd been teasing her before, but there'd been some truth there. He knew exactly what purpose he served for most women and was happy to keep things to one night. Clementine Miller wasn't most women, however, and this was the most enjoyable night out he'd had in months. The fact that it was a fake date didn't change how much real fun he was having.

"If it's not tomorrow, then we'll have to keep going for at least a few weeks." The logic was sound, he knew that, but there was an undercurrent of hope in his words that he couldn't seem to get rid of. "Otherwise, your siblings will run me out of town on a rail if they think I was just messing around with you."

A hum of displeasure echoed in her throat. "What if I was the one messing around with you?"

He laughed, and a few heads turned. From behind the bar, Matt Hayes pursed his lips and raised his eyebrows.

"So are we staying or going?" He gave her a squeeze, hoping it wouldn't be his last chance to hold her like this.

Swiveling her head around to take in all the eyes at the bar, she sighed and leaned into him. "Let's stay."

The call Austin had been expecting since he'd walked into the Floodline hand in hand with Clementine came right as they were leaving.

"It's your sister." He held his phone out to Clementine.

They were almost to his car, and she pulled at his arm to get him to stop in the middle of the parking lot so she could read the name. The heat of her hand on his skin shouldn't have been noticeable beneath their jackets, but despite the early November chill in the air, he felt flushed.

It was probably just from being inside the bar, he reasoned. He hadn't had anything to drink other than water and a milkshake, but Clementine had wanted another beer once they'd decided to stay— this time the raspberry pale ale he knew she loved instead of the stout she'd ordered when Mark had asked. Her eyes were sparkling with the kind of playfulness he'd started to look forward to in the short time they'd been "dating."

"Don't answer." Now her mouth was set in a firm line.

The urge to kiss away that sternness came on him in a rush, as unexpected as a snowstorm in July.

He shook his head. "That'll just make it worse later."

Clementine released his arm and stood up straight, shaking out her hair. "You've known her for years, but I grew up with her. I can handle it."

He smiled. "The time away from Jasper Creek did you some good."

They'd reached his car, and he hurried ahead to open the door for her. She raised an eyebrow. "Chivalrous, are we?"

"Someone might be watching."

Yes, that was the only reason he'd lunged like a champion diver to open her door for her. Not because some sudden, overprotective urge had been creeping up on him all night.

And definitely not because it had felt good to take care of someone again. No, not someone. Clementine. From that first introduction almost exactly three years ago, there were the inklings that she was different. Different from her sister, different from other women. Now it seemed like she was finally realizing the same thing, and instead of hiding away, she was owning it.

Austin was smart enough to see how special she was, how much she trusted him to get her what she wanted, even if she didn't want him.

He was smart enough to not get hurt again.

"What did you mean?" Clementine asked once they were both in the car. He made his way out of the parking lot.

"I mean, if someone was watching us in the parking lot, it would be weird if I didn't hold the door open for you."

He knew what she was referring to, but just like he'd done all night, he wasn't going to give in that easily. Pushing her buttons, getting her to stand up straight and confident the way he knew she could be, was what she needed, not the tender coddling he'd once given her back when she'd worked at Miller Family Medical and she'd been afraid of everything.

Clementine wasn't entirely fearless yet, but another few weeks dating Austin and she'd be bulletproof, just like he was.

She let out an exasperated sigh he knew she used with her siblings but never her parents. "No, what did you mean about my time away from Jasper Creek being good for me?"

"You don't cower as much in front of Anais." He turned onto the side street he knew led to her apartment. "You used to be afraid of her."

"No, I wasn't." She folded her arms across her chest and made a face so contrary he had to laugh.

"Okay, now I see why they call you Minnie. You look just like Bastien."

Austin's phone rang again, and before Clementine could say no, he answered using his car's Bluetooth. "Hey, I'm driving, can't talk."

"Then why did you pick up?" Anais sounded testy, like she always did when she was exhausted. The late nights they'd shared during residency had always been hardest on Austin, but he hid it better.

Plus, he was still ninety-five percent sure his oldest friend was pregnant and either didn't know yet or didn't want to tell anyone.

Austin chuckled, knowing it would annoy Anais even more. "I think it's someone's bedtime."

"Yes, my sister's. Why were you at the Floodline with her?"

"Hey, Nissy." Clementine's voice was strong, but she bit her lip.

"Minnie! Why are you in Austin's car? Where's he taking you?"

"Home. I had a few beers. Where else would he be taking me?"

The other end of the phone was silent. Clementine wasn't a clueless undergrad, and Austin knew it, but Anais still saw her as a little sister, or she wouldn't have called in a panic. There was the ghost of a smirk on Clementine's face. She wanted to make her sister say it out loud.

Oh, she was even more devious than he'd thought. This was going to be fun, for so many reasons he hadn't anticipated.

"Well, from what Isabelle said, it sounded like you two were on a date?" It was clearly supposed to be a question, her voice lifting at the end.

With a conspiratorial glance at Clementine, Austin knew they wouldn't answer that unless she actually asked outright.

"That's weird," he said. "I didn't see Isabelle there tonight."

"Matt called Carter, who called his sister, who called me."

Austin grinned. He'd said all of ten words to Matt about

Clementine, knowing perfectly well it would start the game of telephone that would make its way to the oldest Miller sibling.

Clementine reached forward to mute the call and turned to Austin. "What did you say to Matt?"

Austin shrugged. "He asked if we were on a date, and I said 'have you ever seen me on a date with someone from Jasper Creek?' and he said no. So I shrugged and walked away."

Clementine frowned at this. "Why didn't you just say yes?"

"Because he wouldn't have told Anais in that case."

"That makes no sense."

"If I said yes, he wouldn't have believed me." The logic was so obvious he was surprised Clementine was even asking. Austin didn't date. He took out tourists, had temporary flings with people from out of town, and Matt knew it. If Austin admitted to dating someone, his friend who'd seen him pick up countless women in his bar would see right through him. To leave things vague, it hinted at someone serious that Austin wasn't ready to talk about yet. Matt watched them all night, and the signs were too clear to ignore and not spread around.

Instead of calm agreement, however, Clementine's face had crumpled a bit at his words. Like he'd hurt her somehow. The need to make her feel better swarmed like bees in his chest, driving their stingers in his heart, but before he could say or do anything, she reached forward and unmuted the phone.

"Don't you all have anything better to do on a Friday night than gossip about people?"

"We weren't gossiping, Minnie, we're just concerned."

"If you were so concerned, you'd be out with me and talking to me."

There was silence again on the phone as Anais took in what must be hard to hear from her little sister.

"We'll talk at family dinner next week. You can explain whatever is going on to everyone then."

With a click, the call ended. Austin waited for Clementine to say something, anything, but the uncertain and scared young woman he thought was mostly gone had reappeared. All it took were a few words from Anais, and her walls went right back up. He pulled into her apartment complex's parking lot, parked in front of her building, and turned off the car.

"I take it we'll be going to family dinner together?" In his three years of working with them, and longer being friends with Anais, he'd never been invited. It was a big deal to show up with someone for their family dinners, he knew that, and not something the Miller clan would take lightly.

"It's okay if you don't want to. This wasn't part of the deal."

She was giving him an out, like he had earlier at the bar. If he didn't go, then they could pretend this fake relationship wasn't that serious.

"We don't have to decide now." He reached forward and tucked her hair behind her ear. She closed her eyes like she wanted to savor his touch, and it crushed his heart. "When Anais calls you —and she will—just tell her it's new and we're seeing how things go. I'll say the same thing at work when she asks me. That way, no matter if I show up or not, it still tracks. I don't think your parents will be that bothered one way or another."

She nodded and bit her lip.

"Hey." He tugged at her chin, so she released her lip and looked at him. "Think of it as practice. A few months from now, you'll be telling them about dating Milo, the guy you've loved since you first saw him."

She rolled her eyes. "Love at first sight isn't real. Attraction, yes. You can't deny Mark's an attractive guy."

"Only if you've never seen me in comparison."

This got the laugh from her he'd been aiming for. Her shoulders relaxed and her lips turned up.

"So what made you fall for Miles if it wasn't insta-love?"

She shifted in her seat, the light from the streetlamp catching her hair and making it glow, a dark halo surrounding her thoughtful expression. "He's just so smart and serious, and like, a grown-up, you know?"

He inhaled sharply. Had Mark ever said anything even half as nice about Clementine as she just had about him? There'd been several opportunities to do so tonight, yet Mark had been more focused on observing Austin. Whatever Mark felt for Clementine, it wasn't the same thing as she did for him. That much was obvious.

"He seems like a moron to me, but I guess I can't be right about everything."

"He owns his own clinic and built a new location from nothing in less than a year, Austin. That takes a lot of business savvy. And he's a great PT. The best of anyone I interned with during my program."

A war raged inside Austin's chest. It shouldn't be making him upset to hear all of these things. It was good, really, that she liked this Mark guy for such admirable reasons. It didn't mean he was the right guy for her, but at least she recognized attributes other than physical attractiveness. Though she still seemed blind to just how much Mark's success in Jasper Creek depended on her.

"It's good to hear he's more than just a pretty face. Maybe one day someone will say such nice things about me."

The words were light, like it was a joke, but nothing could be closer to the truth. He ran his hand along the steering wheel and tried to imagine Clementine saying those things about him, but came up blank. For once in his life, his brain didn't want to give him information. Maybe because part of him wanted it so much that to imagine it now would make it too painful when it never happened. Bracing himself for inevitable heartache was the smartest thing to do right now.

"Like your ego needs more boosting." Clementine gave his shoulder a shove, and he laughed like he knew she wanted him to. Her hand lingered on his arm, and he inhaled sharply.

"Indulge me."

She frowned and leaned back in her seat, then licked her lips.

Was she actually thinking about it instead of just throwing back some jab? "I feel safe with you, Austin. I can tell you things I can't tell my family."

His mouth went dry. Yet again, Clementine Miller had surprised him. "So you'll tell me if you don't want to move forward with our plan. You can opt out at any time, you know. Even if it's before the ski trip."

"Don't worry, Austin, I'll go. You just need to make sure I don't fall on my face in front of your whole family."

"I guess our next date will be in the mountains next weekend?"

"Sure, that sounds good." She smiled and grabbed her purse by her feet. "Do I need to get anything to prepare?"

"I'll take care of everything."

"I know you will." With a final smile and a little wave of her hand, she got out of the car.

The trust Clementine had in him was incredible. She was trusting him with her happiness, with not messing this up for her, with making sure she seemed unavailable yet enticing to the one person she really wanted. She trusted him with making sure Mark ended up wanting her too.

So the worst thing Austin could do would be to fall for her.

The boots were on her feet and there were poles in her hands, but Clementine refused to move from her spot in front of the resort's rental shop.

"It'll be fine, Cutie. There's nothing to be worried about."

"Do you know how many people I've treated because of ski injuries?" She wobbled on her ski boots.

In a flash, Austin's hand was on her waist, holding her steady. He gave her one of those smiles. "A few?"

"At least half of our patients this week were once standing right where I am." The clinic had been completely booked, so busy there hadn't been time to talk to Mark about her social media idea or Austin or anything other than work. Though she did manage to mention they'd be skiing this weekend, in passing, just as she left Friday night.

"Where? At the bottom of the bunny slope of the smallest hill in the area?" Austin said, pulling her back to the moment, the heat of his hand burning her hip through her ski pants.

She was sorely tempted to stick her tongue out at him. It was obvious what he was doing. Getting her riled up so her anger and irritation would get her moving.

Pulling away from Austin's hand, she tightened her abs for stability and stomped away in the direction of the ski lift. When she felt balanced enough, she chanced a glare over her shoulder. "You'd better hope Mark doesn't show up."

Mark had said he liked this mountain, and she'd been buzzing all morning at the possibility he might be there. Or at least, she had been until she'd gotten here and seen the size of the slopes. They were so high in the mountains she couldn't even see the top.

"I thought that was the whole point of this plan, for Mark to see you." It barely took Austin a minute to catch up with her. He was carrying her skis but wearing his, gliding along smoothly while she clomped around like an unsteady toddler in her boots.

"Not until I know enough to not look ridiculous."

"Impossible. You look great. The pants especially are quite flattering."

"I look like a marshmallow, Dino."

"So does everyone, Cutie." He stepped forward and laid out her skis. "Come on, before we get in line, you have to put them on."

Her stomach took a dive to the bottom of the mountain. The potential for embarrassment and pain would go up exponentially once she had the skis on her feet. "I can't believe I agreed to do this."

Concern flashed across his face. "Hey, we can go home. No worries." He bent to pick up the skis he'd just put on the ground.

"No, it's fine. I didn't mean it like that." She nibbled her lip.

Whatever this family ski trip was, she knew it was important to him, and she wanted to help him as much as she could. Squaring her shoulders, she let out her breath in a puff of white air and clicked her foot into the ski just like the guy at the shop had shown her. Austin spent a moment checking that her boot was locked in properly.

"Perfect, you're a natural." He flashed her a smile that she felt deep in her gut. "Now try scooting around on one for a minute to get used to it before you put the other one on."

She glanced around, heart in her throat. "No one else is doing that."

"And here I thought you'd be an exemplary student." His lips twitched. "Weren't you the only Miller who had straight As all through high school?"

Warmth spread through her. Who had told him that? There was no way Anais would have said anything. No one ever mentioned the B Anais had gotten in gym her sophomore year, not unless they wanted to see what true fury looked like.

Wherever he'd gotten the information, it worked, and Clementine dutifully pushed herself forward with the foot that wasn't on a ski. After sliding around for a few minutes, Austin proclaimed her a ski-savant. She put on the second ski and they joined the line for the chair lift.

It was a short line, and they were at the front sooner than she would have liked. Austin put a hand on her back so she stayed next to him. "Put your poles in your right hand."

The chair in front of them drifted away, and Clementine looked back to see one coming up behind them, faster than she expected. While her heart hammered away, the chair slid beneath their legs and lifted them off their feet.

"Whoa!" Luckily, she wasn't afraid of heights, but there was something more than a little unsettling about being so high with almost nothing between her and the ground so very far below.

"Hold on to this." He pulled down a bar across their laps. "It takes some getting used to, but you'll do it a lot today."

"Unless I fall on my face the first time down the mountain." Taking a deep breath, she glanced down. Bad idea. Her stomach dropped to the snow-covered valley they were soaring over. "Or I fall off this."

"I won't let you fall." He chuckled. "Have you really never been skiing before? I figured it would be a requirement to graduate from high school out here or something."

"Anais and Bastien got lessons, but they'd moved on to other things by the time I was old enough and interested."

Austin frowned at this. "So you were interested?"

"Well, yeah, but I was interested in lots of things." She'd had to be. It made it easier to go along with whatever her siblings were doing, rather than make a fuss and ask for something she liked. It wasn't until her big decision to go to PT school that she'd finally done something she'd really wanted. Now that she'd had a taste of how freeing it could be to do her own thing, she wasn't sure she ever wanted to stop. Being back in Jasper Creek working and living close to her family was wonderful, but she knew it wasn't what she wanted to do forever.

"Hmm." Austin was still frowning, and her heart thumped in her ears. Even though she hadn't said the last part out loud, she had a feeling he knew. He always seemed to know what she was thinking.

"What about you? Your whole family skis, right?"

"Oh yeah."

"How many siblings do you even have?" With a jolt that could have knocked her off the chairlift, she realized just how little she knew about him. What a terrible fake girlfriend she was turning out to be.

"Pay attention. We're about to get off."

There were still a few chairs in front of them, so he had time to answer. But he didn't want to.

Hmm, what's he hiding?

There was no time for wondering about Austin's mysterious family, however, because skiing took all of her concentration. As kids as young as four sped by her on their tiny skis and mini snowboards, Austin walked her through the basics. Then he walked her through again, because she kept leaning back too far and her skis kept going in opposite directions. Which meant she fell down. A lot.

The entire time he was patient, never frustrated, though still with a slight teasing edge. He called her Cutie more than once, and though it had been irritating at first, it was kind of a sweet nickname. There were many other orange-themed names he could have called her that she had been subjected to over the years.

Finally, after three very slow and cautious runs down the bunny slope, he thought she was ready for something bigger.

"I think you're wrong, Dino."

"Just give it a chance, Cutie. You're stronger than you think."

"Which is not very strong at all, so technically still very weak."

He laughed, throwing his head back in the sunlight, the sound a bright burst of warmth in the midst of the snow.

She liked making him laugh. It was the same feeling she got playing pranks on her siblings, that thrill of joy deep in her belly that let her know she had done something unexpected. Something no one thought she was capable of. Because who would ever think someone like her would be able to make someone like Austin laugh like that?

If Austin saw that as strength, well, then she was definitely stronger than this little bunny slope.

"Fine, lead the way to a green circle."

A few hours later, Clementine was exhausted but happy. It was a wonderful way to spend a day, and she wished she'd insisted on taking lessons when she was younger. She could tell she'd be in pain tomorrow, but it was the good kind, the kind where you used your muscles in a new, fun way, not the kind she'd been worried about. The kind that got you a referral to Vickers Physical Therapy.

Surprise shot through her when she realized she hadn't thought about Mark at all until that moment.

"Should we head back to the lodge for something hot?" Austin was smiling, too, and he seemed to be in the best mood she'd ever seen him in.

Not that he was ever in a bad mood, exactly, but there were days she remembered from working at the clinic, where he'd come in with this sad look on his face, like the world was empty and pointless, though he always hid it as soon as he noticed anyone looking at him. The smile he'd painted on then was different from the one on his face now. This one looked truly happy.

"That sounds like a great idea." Clementine lifted her face to the sky. It was warm in the sun, but she had snow all over her, and despite the marshmallowy feature of her snow gear, there was some moisture that had seeped through to chill her skin.

"Already heading inside?"

At the sound of her boss's voice, she jumped, though not very far, thanks to the skis still on her feet.

"Mark! You're here." She'd actually forgotten she'd talked about this trip to him. It had been such a quick mention, and he hadn't said anything about actually coming, just that he liked the mountain.

"It was too nice a day to not spend some of it skiing. I hoped I might run into you."

Warmth spread through her. He'd listened to her. He was here, *hoping* to run into her.

She glanced at Austin, excited to share in this little triumph, but one quick glance at his face and she cooled off. His smile was gone, replaced with a frosty neutrality she'd never seen before.

"Clementine's never been skiing before, so she needs a break."

Great, they're doing that thing again where they talk about me like I'm not here.

Mark's own features clouded, his eyebrows drawing together, while Clementine's heart thumped wildly in her chest. Whatever was going to happen next wasn't going to be good.

NINE

AUSTIN

"You don't need a break though, do you, Gibson?" Mark's eyebrows were lifted in a not-so-subtle challenge. The sun was glinting off the edge of his obnoxiously expensive ski poles.

"Where are you headed?" Austin gripped his own poles so hard he thought they might bend in two. Between being on the mountain and spending hours with Clementine, it had been the perfect day so far. Only good things ever happened in winter for him. Today was more proof of that.

Then this moron showed up and ruined everything.

"Austin..." Next to him, Clementine's voice was quiet but firm.

He ignored her.

Mark named the most difficult slope on the mountain, one Austin had done several times already. Though not since last winter. "Think you can make it to the bottom before me?"

It was childish, illogical, and possibly dangerous.

But Austin wanted to beat Mark more than he'd ever wanted anything.

"Of course I can. I'll meet you there."

Mark nodded once and disappeared down the path that led to the blacks.

"This is ridiculous," Clementine said as soon as he was gone. "What will beating him down a slope prove?"

"Absolutely nothing, but it'll make him hate me more."

Clementine raised an eyebrow. "I didn't think that was possible after the Floodline."

How to explain that the more a guy hated him, the more he'd want what Austin had without sounding like the egotistical maniac Clementine already thought he was?

He put his hand on her cheek and smirked. "The bigger idiot I look like, the better you look."

She didn't move away from his touch, but she narrowed her eyes, clearly knowing there was more to what was going on than he was telling her. It was only because she wanted Mark so much that she was willing to believe Austin over her own instincts. Because he could get her what she wanted.

"I guess I'll wait for you two idiots down there." She took a deep breath, then looked down the slope they'd been skiing all morning. Her teeth sank into her bottom lip. "I haven't done this by myself yet."

"You'll be fine." He tugged at her lip to free it from her anxious nibbling, more tempted than he'd ever been to kiss her.

Thankfully, she pulled away from him. "Of course I will. I had an excellent teacher."

This lifted his spirits more than he expected it to. There was nothing coddling or patronizing about Clementine. No batting of eyelashes or faking incompetence just to get his attention.

Because they weren't actually dating.

"Will you be cheering me on?"

"Absolutely not."

He chuckled. "So you're rooting for Mark?"

"No. You're both being boneheads."

Laughing harder now, he waved her off, and he made his way over to the blue run. Hopefully the pragmatic pep talk from

Clementine would give him that extra burst of speed to crush her crush.

Which was a totally normal thing to want. Absolutely not an indication that he was developing any kind of feelings for her. That would be a very boneheaded thing to do.

Mark was waiting for him in his over-the-top ski ensemble that was more Switzerland than Colorado. The burning desire to beat him was coursing through Austin's veins, heating him like it was mid-August instead of mid-November. After a curt nod at his opponent, they both got into position and waited for the other to count down. Finally, Austin couldn't wait anymore and just cried "Go!" then pushed off as fast as he could.

It was too easy, he thought, as he bent forward, and the snow-covered trees whipped past him. He hadn't been on this slope since last winter, and he'd spent the whole day with Clementine on the easier one. But his body knew exactly what to do. The Millers weren't the only competitive siblings, and spending every winter in the mountains with his family had perfected Austin's ability to weigh up his options quickly to take every advantage he could.

He looked back and let out a little triumphant laugh when he saw how far back Mark was.

Then he turned back and saw the lift pole, somehow between him and the bottom of the run. The course had narrowed more than he remembered, and the trees that had been blurs before were now surrounding him.

With a twist of his hips, he turned to avoid hitting the trees and the pole, but tilted just a little too far to the right, his left ski lifting off the ground. He swung his arms wildly, pointlessly, knowing he was going to fall and it was going to hurt like hell.

The pain was sharp and instant. His shoulder took the brunt of his weight, and the tug beneath the layers of clothing was like a silent reprimand at his own idiocy.

He was smarter than this. The last time he'd been hurt skiing was when he was a kid, still learning, and eager to go faster than he was ready to. He'd learned his lesson then, but this was something new. Racing his brother and sisters? That was his typical winter holiday. But he'd never been in an unofficial race against the man his fake girlfriend was pining after and he was irrationally jealous of.

There was only a moment alone with his thoughts before some concerned passerby approached.

Of course the voice he heard was the last one he wanted.

"Lost control at the end there, huh, buddy?" Mark's tone could have been interpreted as gentle, the way you'd speak to a little kid. Yet Austin heard the gloating condescension flowing beneath his words like Mark was screaming in his ear. "Those trees look like they snuck up on you. Should we have done this on the bunny slopes instead?"

If Austin's shoulder hadn't been on fire, he'd have punched the guy right there. All he could do now was glare at him as best he could while holding in the groans of pain he so desperately wanted to let out.

There was a crunch of snow nearby, and Clementine's concerned voice floated over him.

"Austin! What happened?"

Now he let the groans out, exaggerating them while keeping his eyes on Mark. It was with grim satisfaction that he saw the other man's expression darken when Clementine knelt beside Austin.

"I swerved so I wouldn't knock down a tree. I'm very strong, you know."

Not even a hint of a smile. Her eyes were wide, as full of concern as her voice was. "Can you move your legs? What hurts?"

His heart thumped in his rib cage. She was really worried.

"It's just my shoulder." He sat up, pushing gently with the arm that wasn't throbbing in agony. A quick internal scan revealed nothing else was in pain, but he let Clementine ask him questions and check him, loving the way it made Mark's scowl deepen.

"It's probably dislocated," the other man said darkly when Clementine had finished her questions. "You should head to first aid."

Austin gritted his teeth, sucking in a quiet breath at the pain. "I'm a doctor. I know when I need first aid. I don't."

"You should let my parents take a look on the way home." Clementine stood, and Austin let her help him up, even though he didn't really need it. The feel of her arm around him was worth as much as winning against Mark would have been.

Then he leaned into her and breathed in her fresh, sunlit smell.

"If you insist, Cutie."

No, he took it back. This was even better than winning would have been.

"Thank goodness you haven't started that social media idea yet, Clem." Mark was smiling, but there was an edge to his voice. "You'll be too busy taking care of this guy in your spare time for anything else."

"Excuse me?" Austin took a step forward, pulling away from Clementine's arm around him. "Why the hell would a woman automatically be responsible for taking care of someone?"

A corner of Mark's lip lifted, and Austin's stomach sank.

"I was talking about her skills as a physical therapist, of course. You'll have my best one treating you."

With that, Mark waggled his fingers in goodbye and wandered off in the direction of the ski lift, shaking his head and smirking.

Well, well, well. It seemed Austin had lost in more ways than one today.

When he looked down at Clementine to apologize, she was clutching his poles and biting her bottom lip. With his good hand, he reached forward and tugged at her chin to release it. The urge to kiss her was still there, but it was buried beneath a hundred other thoughts and emotions. Curiosity being the most predominant.

"What did he mean?"

"I'm sure he doesn't really think I'm his best therapist." It would have been easy to assume her face was red because of the cold, but he knew better. He knew her better. "But you are probably going to need a lot of physical therapy. If it's a dislocated shoulder, they're easy to reinjure."

"No, what did he mean about your social media idea?"

Her shoulders rose with a sharp inhale. This was something she wanted, something important. But unlike deciding to get her PT degree, even though it would upset her family, or going after Mark in the most ridiculous and impractical way by pretending to date Austin, Clementine was hesitating about this.

So he knew it must be *really* important.

"It's nothing. Just something I've been thinking about for the clinic." She reached down to get his skis, but he got there first. He still had one good hand, and even if his shoulder was singing in pain, she was already carrying his poles. He could make it to the lodge and to the car. Loaded down with their gear, she led the way, shaking away the hair the wind had blown into her face. She looked so worried he thought his chest would cave in.

"I can go somewhere else for PT so you have time for whatever it is," he said.

"Don't be ridiculous. Of course I'll take care of you."

There was no resentment in her words, no anger. More like disbelief that he'd ever believed she wouldn't want to do this for him. The searing ache in his shoulder suddenly wasn't quite so bad.

"So what's the idea?"

They crunched through the snow for a few moments, and he wasn't sure if she'd actually answer him.

"Just something for all the office workers I treat. Little videos of stretches they can do during the day." She looked back the way they came and patted her pockets like she was checking she hadn't forgotten anything. Or was looking for a reason to escape this conversation. "I told Mark about it the other week, and he said it was a good idea, but we haven't talked about it again since then. He was probably just being nice and doesn't really want to do it."

Like Austin needed another reason to hate the guy. His new clinic was less than a year old, and he was saying no to a great idea for more publicity? "I'm sure he's just waiting for the right moment."

Mark never had any intention of letting her do the videos, was what Austin was thinking, however. Because why would Mark let Clementine get more attention than him? Why would he let her make her own name for herself when having a Miller working under him was much more to his advantage?

It was becoming more and more obvious to Austin that Mark was absolutely not interested in Clementine romantically. The battle they'd had on the slopes was about power and control. Mark was afraid of losing Clementine's attention, her adoration, her presence at his fledgling clinic. So why didn't Austin just tell her that?

They were at the lodge now, and Austin held open the door with his good hand. Clementine rolled her eyes, but there was a flush of red on her cheeks that he didn't think was from the sun.

"Do you want to hear more about the idea?" Clementine asked as she passed through the door.

"Of course." He followed her inside, victory pumping in his veins. He might have lost the race, but he was the one who could get her what she wanted. Austin was the one who could make her happy.

"Thanks. I want to practice what I'll say when Mark finally asks about it again."

Disappointment whipped through him, shattering his hope, like a broken window that was only ever taped back together. The smallest wind could knock a piece out.

And Clementine Miller was turning into a hurricane.

TEN

CLEMENTINE

Pulling into her parents' house, Clementine felt the panic rise hot in her chest, ashy and dark, like a volcano about to erupt.

As usual, Austin seemed to know what she was thinking.

"Everything will be fine," he said softly, his arm tucked next to his body, held in place with a jacket they'd turned into a makeshift sling.

Clementine flopped back in the driver's seat and peeked at the house she'd grown up in like it was the gates to hell. "Says the perfect oldest child whose parents adore him."

"I never said I'm the oldest."

"You're not?" Clementine turned to look at him, and he had that self-assured yet playful smile on his face. It was like he knew everything she was going to say and going to do but wasn't bored by it. Like it was fun for him.

"I am, but I'm curious how you could tell."

The victory of being right was exactly what she needed to distract her from what they were about to do. Even if part of her knew her parents wouldn't react badly to her dating Austin, it didn't take away the anxiety of having to actually say the words to them.

"You are basically the hot guy version of Anais. Except..." She bit her lip and shifted in the seat. "You're a lot more patient with me than she is."

He blinked, like he hadn't expected her to say that. A different kind of victory whipped through her. Surprising Austin wasn't something that was easy, she knew that.

"I don't think she sees you quite the same way I do," he said, his eyes soft and searching.

She swallowed hard, her seat belt digging into her shoulder as she leaned forward a little. "And what way is that?"

"Like a complete and total menace that would get her fake boyfriend's shoulder dislocated and not even let her doctor parents check it out."

The laugh burst out of her, and the rest of her tension floated away. She shoved him, careful to avoid his injured side. "Excuse me. I do believe I was the one who called you two boneheads. I did not encourage your tree hugging in any way, shape, or form. Why should I help you fix it?"

"Because I'm adorable?" He batted his ridiculously long eyelashes at her. "And, need I remind you, I hurt because I wanted to avoid the tree, not hug it."

With another laugh, she unbuckled her seat belt and opened her car door. "Come on, Dino. Let's get your old bones all patched up."

It wasn't the way she'd planned on telling her parents about dating him, but overall, it went as well as she could have hoped. After taking all of a few minutes to put a proper sling on Austin, her dad spent the better part of an hour talking about things at the clinic. Then her mom jumped in with updates about people Austin knew from his time at Centennial University Hospital, where he'd worked before coming to Jasper Creek.

When she finally managed to speak up, to let them know their day on the mountain had been a date, her parents took the news in stride, without any comment other than they hoped he'd be coming to the family dinner that week.

Clementine was losing count of how many "you were rights" she owed Austin, but she was sure he was keeping track and she didn't have to worry about it.

Which was perfect, since here she was three days later and the idea of family dinner was making her so anxious she thought she might throw up.

As her last patient of the day walked out of the clinic with just a little less pain than when he walked in, Clementine should have been feeling good. She leaned against the mat table, alone in the large treatment room she'd been sharing all day with the other therapists. Everyone else had gone home already, and she was glad for a bit of quiet in the midst of what had been an emotional few days.

Family dinners were the highlights of her week. She got to see her nephew, eat amazing food, and hang out with the people she loved most.

But all she'd been able to think about since leaving her parents' house with Austin's arm in a proper sling was how Bastien would react to seeing them together. He would already know—Anais would have made sure of that. It was something Clementine should have told him herself, she knew that, but if saying the words to her parents had been hard, saying them to Bastien felt impossible.

There was no way he'd actually believe it. Bastien knew her better than any of her siblings, knew what her scheming face looked like, had helped her trick the others countless times in childhood. Any hint of hesitation or pretending he'd spot in an instant.

With a groan that echoed in the empty room, she pressed her back against the mat table and brought her hands to her face. Tonight would be beyond challenging. The stress had been eating away at her all week.

Apparently, the toll it was taking on her was enough that even Mark noticed.

"Everything okay?"

She jumped at the sound of his voice and looked up to find him leaning against the table next to her, a frown of concern wrinkling his perfect face. She hadn't even noticed him coming in because she'd been so wrapped up in her thoughts. He wasn't often in the larger treatment space, too busy in his office with the administration of such a large clinic, or in one of the smaller therapy rooms used for certain cases that needed more privacy. That's when he was in Jasper Creek at all. Which, Clementine realized with a jolt, had been more often than usual the past few weeks.

Because of me?

"Fine. Just worried about family dinner tonight."

"They don't approve of your boyfriend?"

Of all the worries she had, this actually wasn't one of them. Dating a doctor, even if he was technically her dad's employee, wasn't a huge deal. Her parents' reaction this weekend was proof of that. It was almost like they'd expected this from her. After all, it kept her in the Miller Family Medical circle, where Anais had always wanted her to be.

But Mark... he was the departure from all of that. His dark eyes were fixed on hers, concern wrinkling his brow. Bringing him home to meet her family would be the clearest sign she could give them that she didn't want the life they all had. To get closer to the life she wanted with the man standing next to her, first she had to get everyone to believe she was with Austin.

At least Mark seemed convinced.

Clementine tilted her head and raised her eyebrows. "It sounds like you don't approve of him."

"I don't."

He said it simply, like a fact, like this was what anyone else would say.

Clementine's chest heated with an unexpected flare of anger and crossed her arms.

"Is there any particular reason or just normal guy jealousy?"

That's what it was with Bastien, even if he'd never outright told Clementine that. The girlfriend he'd had before Gabby had left him for a doctor. From what she'd seen since she'd been home, even the happiness that he had now with Gabby hadn't totally erased his feelings about Austin.

Bastien and Austin got along well enough, mostly because Austin and Gabby were good friends. If given the choice, however, it was obvious the two men would like to have nothing to do with one another.

"I'm not jealous," Mark said quickly, then chuckled, running a hand over his hair to smooth back a single lock that had fallen out of place. "Not of someone who can't even handle a blue run."

When she didn't laugh along with him, he cleared his throat. "Sorry, that was inappropriate. How's his shoulder doing?"

"It's dislocated—"

"That's what I figured."

If she didn't have four siblings who interrupted her on a regular basis, she might have been upset. Even so, she had to bite back her initial reply, which would have been fine to say to Bastien or Dani, but wasn't a very polite thing to say to her boss.

"No surgery needed, no damage to the rotator cuff. He'll need PT, of course."

Mark shook his head and propped one arm on the table. "It sucks to see someone like him with someone like you, when you could do so much better."

It was a compliment for her, sure, but a major dig at Austin. A warm swell of irritation swept through her, loosening the normally tight tongue she had around Mark.

"I honestly have no idea what you're talking about, so unless you feel like explaining, I have a dinner to get to."

She pushed off the table and walked a few steps toward the

door before he grabbed her arm. "Wait, Clem, I'm sorry. That came out all wrong."

The pressure of his hand on her should have been welcome. This kind of interest and attention from him was something she'd been dreaming of for months. She shook it off, then turned to face him, an eyebrow lifted in expectation.

Mark sighed and rubbed his hands over his face. "You just started dating and already he needs to rely on you, when it should be the other way around."

Was that how he saw her? As someone who needed a man to do things for her? She put her hands on her hips. "I'm perfectly capable of taking care of myself."

"I know. That's not what I meant." He held up his palms in surrender. "I just hear stuff, that's all. He has kind of a reputation."

"I'm aware." It was part of the reason fake dating him was so convincing. Otherwise, no one—especially Bastien—would believe he'd be with her.

"I just don't want to see you get hurt." Mark reached out and squeezed her shoulder. "I don't want to lose my best therapist."

A flush crept across her face and she looked down, her familiar bashfulness returning. "I'm not your best. I just started."

"This place wouldn't have been such a success so quickly without you, Clem."

The warmth in her cheeks made its way south, heating her whole body. She dug the toes of her shoe into the floor. It was such a wonderful thing to hear. She didn't even mind the terrible nickname as much as usual. "Thank you."

"We haven't had a chance to talk about your social media idea yet. Maybe tomorrow?"

Her head shot up, heart thumping hard. This was the first time he'd mentioned it since she'd brought it up, so she'd been sure he'd forgotten about it. But they'd been busy at the clinic, and as the owner, he had plenty of other things to worry about. Maybe this was just the first chance he'd gotten to bring it up.

"Sure, that'd be great."

"Have fun at your dinner." Mark gave her a smile that melted her knees, and he walked over to his office at the other side of the large therapy room.

She was getting so close. Tonight had to go perfectly.

Still floating from the conversation with Mark, Clementine knew she was beaming when she picked up Austin, who wouldn't be able to drive for another week or two.

Once he was in the car, he twisted awkwardly in his attempt to get his seat belt buckled with only one hand, and she reached over to do it for him.

"Thanks," he said, looking at her with that assessing gaze of his. "Good day at work?"

A smile spread wide across her face. "Yes. The plan is definitely working."

He focused his gaze on his seat belt and adjusted it lower on his shoulder. "Oh? Did he say something?"

"He doesn't want me to get hurt by you." She drove down his street, checking her GPS to make sure she was going in the right direction. Austin lived in a larger town next to Jasper Creek. It wasn't too far, but she wasn't in this area often. "He says he doesn't want to lose me, that I'm a great PT."

A frown crinkled Austin's perfect face. "I could have told you that."

"How? You've never seen me work."

"Have you seen me work? You know I'm a good doctor."

"That's because of what I hear."

"Same." His face was still twisted by a frown. "I see all the same people you do but for different reasons. They're thrilled there's another Miller they can go to. I don't think they would have given the clinic a chance if you weren't there."

And just like that, her good mood vanished. She turned left without thinking, and the map on her phone rerouted automatically.

"So Mark only hired me because I'm a Miller?" Her pulse had ticked up a notch at her wrong turn but mostly at his words.

"You can't pretend it wasn't a factor."

Fire burned in her throat. "He didn't know who I was when he hired me as an intern."

"You say he's a smart guy. He would have done his research, found out who the doctors were in the area. What he should have done was reach out to them, but for whatever reason, he didn't. Even if he didn't know who you were at first, it would have been easy for him to—"

"Just stop." She held up her hand. The pounding in her ears made it hard to concentrate. They drove a few minutes in tense silence before she spoke again. "We can't be fighting tonight."

"This is a fight?" At his playful tone, she glanced over at him. He raised an eyebrow and gave her a half smirk. "It's barely a three on the Bastien-Anais scale."

"Don't try to make me laugh right now." She pursed her lips, holding back a mess of emotions.

They were almost on her parents' street, and she'd gone from thrilled to furious to mildly amused so quickly she had emotional whiplash. If Austin were really her boyfriend, she'd never be bored, that was for sure.

If *he were really her boyfriend*? She let out a quiet snort-laugh. Like that would ever happen.

"Making you laugh is what any good boyfriend would do if his girlfriend was mad at him."

She pulled up in front of her parents' house and parked the car. "I thought it's usually flowers or chocolates."

"You've had a boyfriend do that?"

"No, I've never—" Her breath caught in her throat and she glanced at him, heart pounding. If she was going to admit to Austin she'd never had a boyfriend before, then she might as well tell him she'd never kissed anyone, either.

The silence was heavy in the car, and the look on Austin's face was one of the most penetrating he'd ever given her. Like he was reading her mind, digging into her secrets, devouring them like he was starving for them.

Then, suddenly, his face softened, the hungry edge of him disappearing like it had never been there. He reached out and tucked a strand of hair behind her ear. This small bit of contact was enough to set sparks running across her skin, to raise the temperature in the car by several degrees.

"Any jealous ex-lovers I need to be worried about?" His voice was soft, gently teasing her with the same words he'd made her say at the Floodline.

The air in the car was pressing down on her, thick and hot. She could barely whisper her response. "I think you know the answer to that."

"I want to hear you say it."

"Why do you always do that?"

He raised his eyebrows. "Do what?"

"Make me say things out loud that I don't want to say."

Now his lips turned up in that more familiar, sneaky smile. "Because you're stronger than you think, Cutie."

She rolled her eyes at the ridiculous nickname, and he chuckled, the deep vibrations humming in her own chest. Turning away from those piercing eyes, she picked at a loose thread on the leather of the steering wheel. "I've never had a boyfriend before. There, happy?"

"Not remotely, but spending time with you is helping."

The words had been so quiet, Clementine wasn't even sure she'd really heard them. She slid her eyes over to him, but before she could do or say anything in response, he was out of the car and coming around to her side to open her door. He extended his good hand, and she took it, their gloved fingers wrapping together as if they'd been doing this for years instead of a handful of times.

"Ready?"

She let him pull her out of the car, then blew out a white puff of breath in the cold evening air. "Not even a little."

He chuckled again, and her shoulders relaxed at the sound. He closed the door and gave her hand a comforting squeeze.

They could do this. It would be fine. A regular family dinner, just with one extra person. The same as Jackson or Gabby.

Except Austin is only my fake boyfriend.

As they walked up the front steps, hand in hand, she found herself wishing it wasn't fake. That she had a real boyfriend for once, the kind she could laugh with, who said nice things to her, who made her laugh when she was mad.

It was easy, way too easy, to imagine that Austin was that boyfriend.

"It'll be fine," Austin whispered in her ear when they got to the front door. His breath on the side of her face tickled, and she smiled, leaning in a little closer.

Of course, that's the exact moment Bastien opened it. When she saw his glower, her heart leaped into her throat. Maybe she wouldn't have that much trouble convincing him that she and Austin were dating.

"You're late." His eyes narrowed with familiar displeasure.

Maybe that wasn't actually a good thing.

Clementine dropped Austin's hand and hurried forward, brushing past Bastien without looking at him. "No, we're not. We're fifteen minutes early."

There must have been a head nod or some other silent greeting between Austin and her brother, since she heard nothing behind her as she made her way further into the house.

Everything was the same as it had been since she was a teenager, the same family photos and kid art on the walls. She cringed at a particularly bad picture of herself in middle school, braces and glasses and a horrible haircut.

"I never noticed this one before." Heat flooded her at the sound of Austin's voice at her back. Of course this would be the photo he'd see.

He'd been to the house before for parties, but this was the first time he was coming to family game night. What other embarrassing things would he see tonight? Would he think less of her?

Wait, why did she care? It wasn't like they were actually dating.

Not that Bastien suspected that. He came up right behind them, hovering over their shoulders.

"What's the game tonight?" There was a mortifying tremble in her voice she hoped Austin wouldn't hear.

Her brother was fiercely competitive, and so was Anais. Clementine only was when she knew for sure she had a chance to win. The game Bastien had chosen would let her know exactly how competitive he was feeling tonight.

"No game. I thought we'd just have a regular family dinner." He put a hand on both of their shoulders. "Get to know this new boyfriend of yours a little better."

Clementine's stomach dropped. "You've known him for years."

"As a friend," he said. "As a colleague. But not as your boyfriend."

Meaning it was going to be relentless. If it was anything like the dinner she'd told them all she wasn't going to medical school, they'd be here all night.

"I'm an open book, Bastien." Austin turned and gave him one of his smiles, the kind that she'd seen convince patients to promise entire routine changes.

Her brother only scowled in response.

They were herded into the dining room, where Austin was greeted warmly by her father. While Clementine hugged her mom, the two men started chatting, and her father let out a belly laugh at something Austin said.

Though she knew they'd been working together now for almost three years, it was still a relief to see them getting along tonight, in this setting. Even if Austin wasn't really her boyfriend, she would hate to think that him dating her would make things more difficult for him at work. He hadn't mentioned anything happening this week, but maybe Anais was holding off until tonight. Family dinner made things official in a way nothing else did.

Clementine sat down next to Austin, and though he kept talking to her father, he put his hand on hers under the table. Everyone else took their seats, Jackson across from Anais, who was next to Gabby, and Bastien across from Austin, all the better to glare at him. When they started eating, Austin took his hand away from hers, since he only had one good one, but he kept his leg pressed against hers in what she knew was his way of reassuring her. The conversation revolved around how Jamie was sleeping and his latest noises and milestones. Slowly, Clementine started to relax. This was just like any other family dinner but with someone sitting next to her.

Touching her leg with his under the table.

At a lull in the conversation, Jackson glanced at Anais, then turned to Austin. "How's the shoulder?"

"I'll be out of the sling next week and can start PT." He smiled at Clementine. "I've got the best one in town."

Color rose to her cheeks. "That's not even halfway true. Mark —" She hesitated. It felt disloyal somehow to mention his name when sitting next to Austin, his leg brushing up against hers. "Everyone I work with has been doing it way longer than me."

"Yeah, but we didn't start referring people until you started working there," Anais said. "He just came in here, set up shop, didn't reach out to anyone, expecting people to just go there because it was close. That may work in Denver but not here."

It was almost exactly what Austin had said in the car. Fire worked its way up her chest, but the words she wanted to say got stuck in her throat. With anyone else, she could have fought back, just like with Austin earlier. But with her older sister, she was thrust into shy little girl mode, her fight-or-flight response firmly urging her to choose the "run away" option.

Next to her, Austin leaned closer to her, his presence at her side silently encouraging, like he knew what she was thinking and feeling. He probably did. He always seemed to know, especially when it came to Mark and her family.

So it was no surprise that when he spoke before Clementine could gather her courage, it was something very close to what she would have liked to say. "It's not easy to be an outsider in Jasper Creek, you know. A little help early on can make a big difference. We don't all have friends from med school to help."

A slight tinge of red crept up her sister's face as gratitude spread through Clementine, warm and supportive as a hammock in the summer sun. He didn't have to defend Mark, probably wanted to agree with Anais, but he was doing it for Clementine. To everyone else, it just looked like he was defending her boss, but really, he was paving the way so that if Mark was ever here at the table with her, they'd be thinking differently about him.

"So how did this happen?" Gabby wagged a finger between the two of them. "We've all been trying to figure out how."

The change in topic took her off guard, and dread rippled cold and clammy across her skin. Of course she should have expected this question, and when she turned to look at Austin, she tried to convey with her eyes that he should take the lead.

"It's a really cute story, actually." Austin winked at her. "Do you want to tell it, or should I?"

She cleared her throat, not sure what was coming. "Go ahead. You tell it so well."

He smiled, his face calm and smooth. Unlike hers, which must be pale with panic. "I was at the pet store, looking for a puppy for Jamie."

"What?" Bastien's strangled voice cut across the table, and Clementine had to bite the inside of her cheek to stop from snickering.

Oh, this was going to be good. Under the table, she squeezed Austin's thigh to let him know to keep going, that she was on board.

"That's exactly what Cutie said when she saw me there."

"I'm sorry, *Cutie?*" The look of pure revulsion on her sister's face almost made Clementine snort-laugh.

Her mother waved a hand from the head of the table. "Shush, Anais, I'm trying to listen."

"So I'm standing there with a puppy in my arms, trying to figure out what food to buy him, with Clementine next to me, listing all the reasons a dog is the absolutely worst gift for a baby ever."

Now her body was trembling from withheld laughter. He was doing this on purpose to torture her, and if he wasn't also torturing her siblings, then she would have been furious.

From his seat across from Anais, Jackson's lips were turned up, clearly finding as much enjoyment in this as Clementine was. Gabby's attention was focused on Jamie, keeping the little one's hands from grabbing everything on her plate and putting it into his mouth, while her parents were listening with politely interested expressions.

Only Bastien and Anais were glaring at Austin like he was telling them he snuck into her room at night and carried her off into the night like a vampire.

"Since I clearly needed help, I asked if she had any better ideas, and she said... What was it?"

"I think I said, 'only about a million.'" She beamed up at him, like the infatuated new girlfriend she was supposed to be.

He grinned at her, the brightness of it hitting her right in the middle of the chest.

"She was, of course, as she always is, right. And that's how Jamie ended up with a giant stuffed cat and I ended up dating Clementine Miller."

Gabby's eyes lit up. "That is so cute. He loves that cat."

Bastien and Anais both crossed their arms, their lips turned down in identical expressions of displeasure. Clementine's parents and Jackson all had little smiles on their faces, like they wanted to agree with Gabby but were holding off to avoid upsetting the twins.

It hurt more than it should have to see such negative reactions from Bastien and Anais at what was an objectively adorable—albeit completely invented—story. She thought the challenge tonight would be convincing Bastien this relationship was real, but that wasn't what she was worried about now.

While she busied herself with refilling her glass of water, despair trickled into her heart. She wished her older siblings could be on her side right away for once. They loved her, of course they did, but they both had such specific ideas about how she should live her life.

"Just like that. She helps you pick out a gift, and you ask her out?" Bastien shook his head. "Is this a joke or something? Was the Floodline closed that day?"

She could feel Austin's body still next to her. His face had gone carefully blank. Fire flared in her chest, burning out some of her sadness and replacing it with a familiar irritation and anger. She narrowed her eyes at her brother. "What's that supposed to mean?"

"There was nobody else he could ask out? Or has he already gone through everyone else in a fifty-mile radius?"

"Bastien!" both her mother and Gabby cried out at the same time.

Red flashed in front of Clementine's eyes, and for the first time in her life, she wanted to physically hurt her brother. She knew he didn't get along great with Austin, but this was beyond rude.

"It's fine," Austin said. Clementine turned to see his expression had turned to steel. "I know how to reassure him."

Her stomach dropped.

He was going to tell them all the truth.

Austin lined up his knife so it was perfectly straight next to his plate before he lifted his gaze across the table to where two bright green eyes were drilling into him. Bastien Miller was not a complicated guy. He loved his family, was completely obsessed with Gabby—thanks in no small part to Austin's careful interference last summer—and so proud of his baby son that it was almost physically painful to look at him sometimes.

Bastien also hated Austin for being everything he wasn't: a doctor, a colleague to his sister and wife, an outsider who came in and won over the people in his town. Even if they managed to get along for Gabby's sake, he would probably always hate Austin just a little.

So it was with the extreme patience of someone who had predicted exactly what would happen at tonight's dinner that Austin cocked an eyebrow and replied to Bastien's audaciously blunt question.

"When you've dated as much as I have, you know an incredible woman when you find one." He put his hand on top of Clementine's that was resting on the table. "I know perfectly well your sister is too good for me. And I thanked my lucky stars when she said yes to the most ridiculous request she's probably ever heard."

There was complete and total silence around the table. Next to him, Clementine's breath hitched, and the muscles in her hand tightened beneath his. He was laying it on pretty thick, but nothing he said was a lie. That's what made it so powerful, so believable.

After a few minutes of tense stillness, Clementine's mother cleared her throat and glared at Anais and Bastien.

"Well, if the two of you are quite finished with your ridiculous questions, maybe we could have dessert and talk about something more interesting than your sister's dating life?"

It was meant to be a way to chastise the two oldest Millers, but Austin heard the tremble in the breath Clementine let out. He had assumed the mild reaction from her parents that weekend at the news they were dating hadn't been that unusual. She was, after all, the middle child of five, and a certain amount of parental laxness was to be expected.

But this was something else. If her own mother didn't think her dating life was worth delving into, while her older siblings reacted like she was doing something illegal by bringing him here, no wonder Clementine had never had a boyfriend before. No wonder she'd never asked for skiing lessons as a kid.

The Millers were a warm, loving family. That didn't mean they fully understood just what an extraordinary woman Clementine was. They definitely weren't the ones who were going to help her see that about herself. That was his job, and even if it was temporary, there was nothing fake about how he saw her. How he felt about her.

Dessert was quick, and Austin declined the offer of coffee. No need to make Clementine suffer any longer than necessary. While things had gone roughly as well as he'd anticipated, she was a wreck, barely speaking, her leg jiggling underneath the table so hard he was surprised her teeth weren't chattering.

Out in the car, he waited for her to say something but realized she needed him to go first.

He turned toward her as much as he could with his arm in a sling and the seat belt digging into his hips. "Well, that was almost as fun as dislocating my shoulder."

Clementine, however, didn't even crack a smile, her hands trembling on the steering wheel. "I don't think we should go on a date this weekend."

His stomach dipped. "Already breaking up with me? I thought I did okay tonight."

Maybe he'd overstepped with what he said to Bastien. Maybe she thought he'd been lying.

Maybe, like Cassidy, she'd realized she didn't want to waste any more time pretending when what she really wanted was something else entirely.

At least this time Austin knew going into things he wasn't what her heart truly desired. That didn't mean it wouldn't still hurt like hell.

"You were amazing." She pulled to a stop at a red light and looked at him. The smile she gave him was small, but it lifted his heart. "It was just a lot, the Floodline, then skiing, and now this. And you can't do much with that sling."

"I can still drink at the Floodline with a dislocated shoulder." He raised an eyebrow.

"Yeah, but we've done a lot together lately." There was a curve in the road, and while she leaned to the side, he'd known it was coming and held himself straight. The faintest hint of her shampoo hit his nose in a burst of crisp citrus. "You could probably use a break."

Clementine was the one who needed a break. It was clear as day on her face. For whatever reason, the timid Clementine was sneaking back, and that's the last thing Austin wanted.

He wanted the Clementine he'd been hanging out with the past few weeks, the one who fearlessly tackled new challenges and could easily talk him out of buying a puppy for an infant. The story might have been a fabrication, but it absolutely could have happened. The feelings behind it were as true as anything.

Not that he could tell her that. After everything he'd said tonight, the crush she'd had on him when he first arrived in Jasper Creek—the one that had made it almost impossible for her to talk to him when they'd worked together—might be on the verge of reemerging. Confusing her when she was so set on wanting someone else was something he'd sworn he'd never do again. Cassidy had spent months hesitating, drawing out the pain for both of them. A clean break was always better.

She pulled up in front of his condo and parked. Her request hadn't been a question, but he needed to give her an answer.

"If you're sure, then I'm fine if we don't have a date this week." He drummed the fingers of his good hand on his thigh, the skin still tingling from where she'd squeezed it during dinner. "I want to make sure I'm holding up my end of the bargain."

"You are. Don't worry." She leaned over to unbuckle his seat belt for him, her dark waves, the color of chestnut tonight, brushing against his face while he fought the urge to run his fingers through it. Would he ever get the chance to do that? She sat up straight and smiled at him. "Thanks, by the way. For what you said about Mark. You didn't have to do that."

"I know."

"So why did you?" Clementine raised an eyebrow. When he shifted in his seat, he bumped his shoulder, and she reached out to adjust his sling with gentle hands. "You never do anything without a reason, without thinking through all the possibilities."

"Never say never." The warmth of her hands had spread through his chest. A harsh chuckle escaped him, and there was a sharp stab in his injured joint. "My dislocated shoulder would prove that's not always true."

He raised his eyes to meet hers, and the breath caught in his throat at the intensity of her stare. The small space of her car was hot, though she'd turned off the heater along with the car. Everything about her was enticing him to reach out, touch her, make her forget all about Mark. From the way she was staring at him, like she was looking into his soul, she was halfway to forgetting him already.

"Well, whether you had a reason or not, thank you." Her eyes fluttered and her breath caught.

Oh yeah, they definitely needed a break.

Pulling his eyes away from her was almost impossible, but he managed to turn, hand on the door, ready to escape whatever this was becoming before it went too far.

"Let me know when you take the sling off, and I'll take a look at what you might need in terms of next steps."

"Thanks, Cutie."

She glanced over at him, and he hoped she saw the nickname for what it was: both a peace offering and a promise. Her lips twitched.

"Don't run into any more trees this week, Dino."

The next day, Clementine got a text from Austin right as she walked into work.

NO TREES TODAY.

The grin that spread across her face was as unexpected as her desire to write back immediately. The break she'd so desperately needed last night seemed silly this morning. What she probably needed more than anything was a break from her family. But that was about as likely as Austin falling for her for real.

IT'S ONLY NINE A.M. LET'S SEE IF YOU CAN MAKE IT ALL DAY.

He responded with a picture from the reception area of Miller Family Medical that showed the trees through the front window. The view was a familiar one; he must have been standing right behind her old desk—Hunter's desk now.

I'LL ASK HUNTER TO LET ME KNOW IF ANY OF THESE GUYS MAKE A MOVE.

The snort-laugh that burst out of her was the least attractive sound she'd ever made in her life, so of course, when she looked up from her phone, Mark was standing right in front of her.

"Everything go okay last night?" He raised an eyebrow and

leaned against the doorframe of the break room. The olive of the clinic's scrubs was the perfect color to set off his eyes, and his skin was unusually tan for this time of year. In a word, he looked incredible, but the excitement in Clementine's stomach at the sight of him was barely a flutter compared to what she'd felt from Austin's text.

"Totally fine." She gave him a smile, but he still had a funny expression on his face.

"It really is nice to see you laughing so much, even if it's because of Austin." He held up a hand like he wanted to put it on her shoulder, then let his arm drop by his side. "I just hope he doesn't make you cry later."

It was such an odd thing to say, Clementine didn't even know how to respond. She stood there for a moment, watching him walk away, her stomach a swirling mess of uncertainty. It was incredible that Mark seemed to care, but there was a not-so-small tendril of annoyance that he was commenting on her relationship, just like her siblings had.

Even if it was a fake relationship.

It was starting to feel less fake the more time that went on, even if they weren't seeing each other in person.

Every morning Austin sent her another picture of the front window at the medical practice from behind the reception desk, with a note that the trees hadn't moved yet.

They got snow that week, and the view changed, the branches covered in icicles that glittered in the sun. Now that she worked inside the treatment room all day, she missed having a view of the outside. It was her first winter back in Jasper Creek in two years, and it felt like she was missing her favorite season.

Once again, Austin seemed to know just what she needed without asking.

By Friday, she was seriously considering rescinding her request that they not see each other that weekend. If someone made her this happy, why deny herself that just because she was worried he would never feel the same?

When she walked into work, she was working through in her head exactly how she should phrase her desire to see him without it sounding like she liked him. So consumed by her thoughts, she didn't notice the entire staff was gathered in the middle of the treatment room until Mark called her name.

"Thanks for joining us, Clem."

She looked around, the five other therapists standing in a circle with Mark in the middle. She slipped her phone into her pocket and joined them, cheeks heating. She wasn't late, but with everyone's eyes on her as she took her place next to a colleague, it felt like she'd done something wrong.

"Great." Mark clapped his hands and looked around the circle, a half smile on his mouth. "Now that you're all here, I can tell everyone at once. We've blown past all my expectations for this place. We've already reached my target for new patients that I set for the second half of the year, and it's not even Thanksgiving yet."

Everyone clapped, including Clementine. This was incredible news, and she was so proud that she'd been able to help so many people in such a short amount of time.

"No need for anything fancy, no doing silly dances on social media, just good old-fashioned word of mouth."

The words hit Clementine like a punch in the gut, and her smile froze on her face. He hadn't said her name, and his gaze conveniently skipped over hers as he looked around at his staff, but the barb was clear as day. He hadn't even heard her whole idea, had never found the time to ask her for more details. It had nothing to do with silly dances, but she knew it was a good idea. And not just because Austin had said so when he'd listened to her entire pitch after skiing last weekend.

"To celebrate, I want to take you all out somewhere fun tonight."

"Oh, can we go to the Floodline?" Melissa asked. The others

nodded, looking excited. "Their boozy cookies-and-cream shake is to die for."

"I was thinking somewhere unique. Somewhere special." Now his eyes did meet Clementine's, and he gave her a small, private smile.

Twisty, snarled emotions caught in her chest. Was he trying to make up for the social media comment?

It was exhausting, figuring out what message he was trying to send her. At least with Austin, she knew where she stood. They weren't really dating, and never would. Mark's interest was the whole point of fake dating, so she should be thrilled at this sign of progress.

"There's an ax-throwing bar a few towns over that I've been to a few times. It should be a lot of fun." Everyone let out appreciative noises. "I wanted to see if tonight or tomorrow is better for all of you."

Everyone started talking at once, but the overall consensus seemed to be that night. Luckily, someone else asked if they could bring their partners or spouses.

"Let's keep it just the team. You all work hard and deserve to celebrate together." His lips ticked up in one of his super-wattage smiles. "And I don't want anyone getting hurt and taking you away from the clinic."

Again, his eyes avoided Clementine's, and she knew this comment was directed at her. She was important to him, that much was clear, but Clementine wasn't sure it was for the reason she wanted it to be.

After agreeing on a time to meet there, they all went back to work. Her phone buzzed while she was checking equipment. Austin had sent a picture of the trees in front of the office again, accompanied by an unexpected message.

I'M AROUND TONIGHT IF YOU WANTED TO DO SOMETHING. JUST HANG OUT, NOT A DATE.

It was the perfect way to ask. Exactly what she would have written if SHE'D HAD MORE TIME TO THINK ABOUT IT.

HEADING TO A BAR WITH EVERYONE AT WORK. CELEBRATING A BIG MILESTONE.

CONGRATS! I'M SURE YOU WERE THE REASON THE CLINIC HIT IT. HAVE FUN.

With a pang, she wondered if that would even be possible without Austin next to her.

"Having fun?"

Clementine looked up from her mediocre beer that she kept wishing was ice cream to see Mark leaning on the high table in the corner where she'd hidden herself away.

"Absolutely." Her smile was as fake as the wood paneling on the walls. For the better part of an hour, she'd been standing around—because of course this place didn't have chairs—watching her colleagues and Mark get progressively drunker while throwing axes at a target that was purposely angled to make it impossible to hit the middle and win free beers for a month. Feeling alone in her misery, it was tempting not to take pictures to send to Austin so he could laugh along with her at the cheesiness of it all.

"I love it here." Mark's eyes were shining bright, and she had to admit he looked thrilled. "It's not like any other bar, right? It's special here."

Warmth spread through her chest. He had to be referring to their conversation at the Floodline, this time there was no doubt. It was a shame this place was special for all the wrong reasons.

This wasn't something she could say to Mark, of course. "Thank you again for taking us all out." She took a sip of her beer, the one local brew they'd only had in a can, and gave him another smile, this one a little more genuine. Even if she didn't like it here, it was a nice gesture for him to have done something like this for his staff.

"Of course." His hand was suddenly on top of hers, and he was looking into her eyes with such inebriated earnestness that she had to bite her lip to keep from laughing. His skin was warm and clammy, and instead of enjoying it the way she always thought she would, it was just... there. "I am sorry the social media idea won't work."

Slowly, she pulled her hand away and frowned. "You haven't even heard it."

He shook his head and wobbled a little. Would he even remember having this conversation with her? "It's just not our target clientele. I should have told you earlier but..."

"But what?" There was an edge of anger to her voice that she was sure he couldn't hear.

"You can't leave, Clem." He slumped forward on the table, head in his hands. "I can't do this without you. And that asshole Austin is going to hurt you and then you'll leave."

Heart beating fast, she inhaled as slowly as possible. It wasn't quite the declaration of love or even like that she thought she wanted from him, but it wasn't quite nothing either.

So why was her first instinct to run?

Barely six months into her career and she already knew that she wanted to be more than just someone's employee. Learning would take time. With so many doctors in her family, she knew that better than anyone.

But she knew enough that someone with Mark's experience and knowledge shouldn't be so dependent on someone so new to the field.

The crushing disappointment hit her in the middle of the chest, harder than any of the axes whizzing around the bar. Her sister and Austin had been right. Even if Mark hadn't said it, there was nothing else he could mean. Having a Miller on staff was what he liked about her.

Oh, she knew she was a good PT as well. But she certainly wasn't his best. Only the most important to his business. That didn't mean he couldn't also have feelings for her, but if he had, wouldn't tonight have been a good opportunity to show them? The only feeling she'd gotten from him was that he hated Austin, because if they broke up, he'd lose his most important piece of marketing.

"I'm not going anywhere," Clementine said, her voice hollow. Not that Mark would notice or remember. "I'm happy in Jasper Creek."

For now, at least. All because of Austin, who Clementine hadn't been able to stop thinking about all night.

Mark smiled blearily at her and wandered off to throw more axes. As she watched him joke and laugh with her colleagues, her phone buzzed with a message.

HAVING FUN?

Her lips ticked up in a true smile, the first one of the night. She snapped a quick picture of an empty target, making sure to include the beer can and as much of the decor as she could.

WHAT DO YOU THINK?

When she got a laughing GIF in return, she felt bold enough to tell him the truth.

I WISH YOU WERE HERE. I MISS YOU.

Then she held her breath, waiting for his answer. Three little dots appeared, then disappeared a few times before she finally got a reply.

DOES THAT MEAN WE'LL HAVE A DATE THIS WEEKEND?

She inhaled sharply and looked around the bar. For what, she wasn't sure. Confirmation that she hadn't imagined the message. Confirmation that it didn't mean what she thought it did.

All she got was the drunken laughter and a lungful of humid, dead air that all bars except the Floodline seemed to have. She'd never complain about their remodel ever again after tonight.

Thinking through things logically, the way she was sure Austin had, she remembered that she was the one who had asked for a break. Her words made it sound like she'd changed her mind. So he'd assumed she'd want to go out this weekend.

What had changed, however, was how she felt about Mark.

And Austin.

If there was little chance of Mark developing feelings for her, there was even less that Austin would. Fake dating his friend's little sister to help her was one thing. But she'd never even had a boyfriend before, while he'd been with so many people. There was no way someone like her would be what he wanted. To have fun with, sure. To laugh about the ridiculousness of axe throwing, of course. This was a business transaction. He was helping her get what she wanted, and she was going on his family ski trip. Even though things with Mark hadn't worked out how she wanted, that didn't mean she'd go back on her end of the deal.

It would just make it awkward if she told him she might be developing real feelings for him. He was so observant he'd notice right away that she was acting differently around him. A date this weekend, even if it was what she wanted more than anything, would be a mistake.

NOT THIS WEEKEND, NO. CALL ME WHEN YOUR SHOULDER IS CLEARED FOR PT.

She let out a breath and leaned against the table. Now there was no way he'd interpret things wrong. Her secret was safe.

For now.

Austin was in a terrible mood. He stalked around the break room at Miller Family Medical, throwing open cabinet doors, rifling through drawers, looking for something to help with the pain in his shoulder.

The pain in his chest was something else entirely.

It had been a week since he'd last seen Clementine, and she'd made it clear they wouldn't see each other again until it was time for PT for his shoulder.

Of course the damn thing was taking longer than average to heal. Every morning he checked it before putting on his sling, and there was still the telltale twinge of tightness and pull of muscles that meant he wasn't ready for rehabilitation. There was no reason for him to call Clementine.

It wasn't because he wanted to see her. Or rather, he did want to see her, but not because she was his fake girlfriend. They were real friends, and he didn't want to get that complicated by developing feelings for her.

Finally, he found a bottle of ibuprofen in the back of a drawer. He popped two in his mouth and stormed out of the room, heading for the reception area. Apparently no one had explained to Hunter the importance of keeping a stocked first aid kit in the staff room.

Luckily for Hunter—and unluckily for Austin—Anais was coming out of her office, and when she caught sight of his face, she stopped him in the hallway.

"Trouble sleeping, Gibson? You look tired." She raised an eyebrow, her tone less indulgent than it would have been with anyone else.

There'd been no mention of family dinner all week, but he knew she was still irked about it. The extreme politeness she'd been using with him was like a flashing red light telling him she was still mad, but she didn't want their personal drama to interfere with work. Which he didn't either, normally.

But today his shoulder hurt, and he didn't know when he'd see Clementine again.

"This is a doctor's office. We should be able to find pain medication if we need it."

"You know that's not how it works. We can't just take things if they could impact our work." She crossed her arms and gave him her haughtiest know-it-all look, one he hadn't seen since those first weeks of residency together when he'd deserved it.

Today he definitely didn't.

"My shoulder throbbing also impacts my work." When he matched her glare with one of his own, she sighed and pulled him by his good arm into her office and shut the door.

Whirling on him, her eyes were sparking like he hadn't seen since the time he'd gone out with her roommate and hadn't called back. The protective instinct was strong in Anais, and it would be doing double duty now that she was expecting, even if she didn't realize it yet. "Well, maybe you should have thought of that before taking my baby sister skiing."

"Danielle is younger than Clementine."

"Only in age. Minnie's been more sheltered."

"And whose fault is that?"

There was a pause, then they both said "Bastien" at the same time and burst out laughing.

Shaking her head, Anais walked over to her desk and opened a drawer. "Look, I'm sorry about your shoulder. I should have asked earlier this week how you were doing." She held out a bottle of acetaminophen. "Here. It's the only thing I have on hand right now, but I can ask Hunter to get something else if you need it."

Despite the simmering tension between them, a tremor of victory ran through Austin's chest. Of course that's all she'd have on hand. Pregnant women shouldn't take ibuprofen.

He held up a hand to wave away her offering. "Thanks. I found something in the kitchen."

With a sigh, Anais flopped into the chair behind her desk and ran a hand through her hair. "Is it really hurting that much? Do you need to go home?"

He sat down across from her, worry knotting in his stomach. He noticed for the first time that she wasn't wearing much makeup. There was a gauntness to her cheeks that hadn't been there at family dinner last week. "No, but do you?"

Her eyes glanced left and right before landing on his. "No. I'm fine."

"Anais, please don't lie to me. You know I'm smarter than you."

This had the intended effect of narrowing her eyes and her back straightening. Having her challenge him would be a good distraction from her first-trimester misery. "According to who?"

"Everyone."

Anais twisted her mouth, and displeasure radiated from her. "I can't go home. We're understaffed as it is."

This wasn't how Austin had been interpreting the recent increase in patients, but to Anais, he could see how it might feel that way. "I think we're doing okay. It's always a little busier in winter with all the viruses going around. As long as none of us get sick, then we should be fine until we break for Christmas."

The clinic was closed the week between Christmas and New

Year's, an unusual move but one that Miller Family Medical had been doing for decades, so there were no surprises for the town. Dr. Miller was on call for patients if needed, and in the three years that Austin had been working there, he'd only been needed a handful of times.

"One of us has already gotten sick." She gestured at his arm. "Not sick but waylaid. And my dad really should be thinking about retiring. We should hire another doctor. By the spring, if possible."

It was hard to keep the amusement at her mental gymnastics off his face, but Austin did his best. "I think that's a good idea. If it'll help you feel less stressed."

"I'm stressed because I can't figure out why all of a sudden you and Clementine are together."

"Well, we can't all fall for our sibling's best friend while they're in town."

He could tell she wanted to stick her tongue out at him but was resisting. They were, after all, very professional doctors. "Did you really almost buy Jamie a puppy?"

"What do you think?"

She hesitated, twisting in her chair and making his heart stutter. It reminded him of that night with Clementine when she'd agreed to this fake dating idea. So much had happened since then, in the few short weeks since their agreement. So much had changed, and not just his shoulder. He'd wanted to be less bored. He'd wanted excitement.

He hadn't wanted a split with Anais, one of his best friends.

"I think she's always had a crush on you, and you have to be careful."

Though he'd known about Clementine's crush from the moment he met her, warmth still spread through him to hear it confirmed. The warning in Anais's voice was also clear.

"Sometimes it takes a while to realize what you want. We're not all like you, driven and decisive from the age of five."

The words were intended to placate Anais, but as soon as he said them, he realized he'd been lying to himself for the past week.

He wanted Clementine. For real. This fake dating was leading to some very strong emotions he couldn't quite identify. Being around her felt unlike anything he'd experienced in the past. Whatever these feelings were, he knew he wouldn't be satisfied much longer with only two dates a week and long breaks like they were on now. He wanted to see her.

The compliment still did what he wanted it to, of course. Anais perked up, and the smallest of smiles tilted her lips up. "I *am* sorry you got hurt skiing. Seriously, let me know if you need anything from me, okay?"

The tension in Austin's shoulders relaxed. Even if it still hurt, even if he was now awash in strange new feelings that he hadn't anticipated experiencing for anyone ever again, at least things were back to normal with Anais.

Not normal enough to talk to her about Clementine, of course, but that wasn't really what he needed from her.

"Thanks." He reached his good hand across the desk and gave hers a squeeze. "I'll be fine."

He wouldn't be fine until he saw Clementine again, but that, like so much about what was happening with her, was completely out of his control.

Exactly two weeks after he hurt himself, Clementine got a text from Austin telling her he'd taken off the sling. The anticipation and excitement that rushed through her when she read the words made her lightheaded. Luckily, she was at home, sitting on her couch with Marbles and not at work. The same spot she'd been in every night that week, wishing she hadn't been quite so decisive in her choice to not see him until she had figured out her feelings.

With shaking fingers, she arranged for him to come by her apartment the next day so she could evaluate him. He'd have to see someone else for any actual PT since the clinic's rules strongly recommended therapists not treat their own friends or family, but it seemed only fair that since he'd hurt himself as part of helping her, that she could do him this favor.

She was also out of reasons to avoid seeing him.

It was the first time she'd had a guy over to her place. Ever. She'd never even had a friend over to her parents' house during high school. Her hands were shaking when she opened her door and ushered Austin inside.

"This is a nice place." His eyes took in her secondhand couch and Swedish big box store furniture as he handed her his coat. "Very clean."

He gave her a look like he was trying not to laugh, and she bit her lip. Of course he'd guessed how much time she'd spent getting the space ready for his visit. The fit of cleaning that happened in the twenty-four hours before he arrived was the most intense she had ever done. Marbles had hidden under the bed the entire time, the sound of the vacuum cleaner almost constant.

"Bastien sometimes complains about the cat smell, so I may have gone a little overboard."

"I love cats. I don't mind at all. Bastien should have his nose checked, there's no smell." He looked around again. "Marbles, right? Where is he?"

There was a stutter in her chest, and she squeezed the door handle still in her hand. She closed the door and turned to face him, cheeks flaming. He'd remembered her cat's name.

"He's mad at me because of all the cleaning." They were standing in her entryway, the smallest space in her apartment that she'd made even smaller by putting a table for her keys and shoes. She couldn't quite figure out how to invite him in further without touching him. There was a way Austin moved her around when they were in public, putting his hand on the small of her back, that let her know he was there without feeling like he was guiding her, like she was still in charge. Should she try that with him?

No, better not touch him at all until I have to.

"He'll come out eventually. Once he gets used to you, he's very friendly."

With a smooth stride, Austin stepped around her and toed off his shoes. "Sounds familiar." He nudged his shoes next to hers under the table, then leaned back against the door.

Clementine swallowed hard, her head spinning at the sight of his tall frame in her apartment and his shoes sitting so close to hers. He was here as a patient, she reminded herself. She wasn't sure if he was also here as her fake boyfriend.

"If you were here for real, what would you think?" She took a step backward and bumped into the wall. If they didn't get out of the entryway soon, she was going to combust.

"Am I not really here?" He patted his chest, unbearably muscled beneath the short-sleeved shirt she'd asked him to wear.

"You know what I mean."

He crossed his arms and raised a single eyebrow, his voice rumbly in the small space. "I want to hear you say it."

She rolled her eyes and blew out a breath. "If you were my real boyfriend, and this was the first time you were coming here, what would you think?"

"That it shouldn't have taken three weeks to get me here."

Her entire body shivered. Annoyed that she'd let him see what his words had done to her, she turned on her heel and led the way out of the entryway, toward the living room. "If you're not going to be serious, then just forget it. I'll set up an evaluation for you with one of my colleagues."

"I am being serious." He grabbed her arm, loosely, more to get her to look at him than to actually stop her. When she turned, he was giving her that look again, the one like there was nowhere else he'd rather be. He'd never done it when they were alone before. "If I were really your boyfriend, I wouldn't have waited three weeks to finagle an invitation back here."

"Finagle? Who talks like that? You really are a dinosaur." She gave a weak chuckle, heat swirling in her stomach.

There was no one around. There was no reason for him to say these things unless he really meant them. The dangerous pull of desire that had almost disappeared since first meeting him a few years ago had flared into life again, like a smoldering fire given the tiniest bit of fuel.

Austin's lips curved up, and he leaned toward her like he knew exactly what she was thinking. "Luckily you have experience treating geriatric patients, so I should be fine."

She let out a breath slowly and pulled away from him. This

would be so much easier if he weren't so charming, so sweet, so...
Austin.

"Let's get started then." She led him to the mat she'd set up in the middle of her living room floor.

Once he was lying down, his deep blue eyes met hers, and she suddenly forgot what she was supposed to be doing. She blinked and shook her head.

"Um, let's see how your mobility is doing."

She took his arm by the elbow and slowly moved it around, his skin warm beneath her hands. He never took his eyes off hers.

We should have done this at the clinic.

Or at least she shouldn't have told him to wear a sleeveless shirt. It was to better access his shoulder, of course, but between the shirt and his shorts there was simply too much of him visible.

"I have a question for you, Cutie."

She smiled. The nickname was the perfect way to break the tension, and her own shoulders relaxed as she continued with her examination of his. "What is it, Dino?"

Marbles appeared at his feet, and he was momentarily distracted as the cat wound its way around his legs, purring in a way he never did with Clementine. She bit the inside of her cheek. So much for being afraid of new people.

Austin smiled down at the cat as Clementine continued to test the mobility of his shoulder. Then he squeezed his eyes shut like he was in pain, and she instantly stopped what she was doing with his arm.

"Oh no, did I hurt you?"

"Only with your terrible nickname." His eyes blazed open, and her heart leaped into her throat. "But yeah, that last thing did kind of hurt."

She swallowed hard and focused on the steps she'd gone through dozens of times already with patients of all ages. The familiar routine relieved some of the anxiety thrumming in her veins, but only some. At least Marbles had wandered off again, back to his cave under the bed. "Things don't look too bad. You shouldn't need much PT, but you should still come in and see someone at least a few times."

"There's nothing you can show me now?"

There were lots of things she wanted to show him, but none of them had anything to do with his shoulder.

She cleared her throat. "Let's head to the wall. There are a few exercises you can do there. But go easy until someone puts a full plan in place for you."

Unlike the PT clinic, her living room didn't have the same open wall space, and Austin had to stand right next to her. Their arms brushed as she showed him the first exercise, and he put his hand on her hip to move her out of the way so he could do it.

The pressure of his hand was like fire, heating through her and stealing her breath.

Definitely should have done this at the clinic.

"Are you okay?" he asked softly, his head just a few inches away from hers. "I can tell you're thinking hard about something."

"Just that I don't really have the space for this here. We should have done this at the clinic." She shifted her hips to put some space between them, but he mirrored her movement, and they stayed much closer together than she would ever have been with a regular patient.

"If we did, people would expect to see us kiss."

"Would they really?"

He brought his hand to her face and brushed away a few strands that had fallen out of her ponytail. "Not, like, fully making out in front of everyone. But at least a little something."

With his palm on her cheek, the scene was easy to imagine, and she closed her eyes to savor the picture of his lips on hers. She had a harder time imagining what it would feel like.

"I never have before."

The words slipped out without thinking, and her eyes wrenched open in a sickening realization of what she'd just said.

The look of shock on Austin's face wasn't one she'd ever seen before. His hand dropped from her face.

"You mean you've never made out with anyone in the clinic before?" he asked like he already knew the answer but was hoping he was wrong.

Except Austin was never wrong, was he?

"No, I've never kissed anybody... ever." She looked away, turning against the wall slightly to avoid seeing his shock turn to pity.

There was only the sound of his breathing, heavier than she'd have expected, but it was hot in her living room. It just kept getting hotter the longer they stood there, close but not touching, his eyes burning holes in her turned away face.

"Would you like to practice?"

"What?" She whipped her head around, expecting to see his perfect mouth curved up in a smirk or a teasing glint in his eyes. Instead, he was the softer version of Austin that always seemed to pop up exactly when she needed it. The Austin with a patient look in his eyes that made her wish this wasn't all pretend.

"I'd be happy to kiss you as much as you'd like." His whole body tensed for a moment, then he cleared his throat and his shoulders dropped. "What I mean is, if the point of all this is to get you ready to date Mark, then that includes making sure you know how to kiss."

At the sound of her boss's name, the man she'd been crushing on for months until she realized he only saw her as a meal ticket, she took a step back. Or tried to, at least, but she was already against the wall, so she pushed back into it, her heart pounding and hands sweating.

If this was really for Mark, then it would have been easy. It would be a nothing kiss with Austin, just pretend, just practice, like he said. But her breathing was short and fast, and her body was trembling. This wasn't easy, because she wanted it to be Austin. Not as practice. But for real. For now, everything she'd realized the night at that ridiculous axe-throwing bar had been kept to herself. What if she told Austin she didn't want it to be just practice and then he didn't want to do it anymore?

Somehow, in the churning turmoil of her body, she managed to speak. "That sounds like a good idea."

"Yeah?" There was a flicker in his eyes and the slightest hint of surprise in his voice.

"You're the expert, after all, aren't you?"

Instantly his face went dark, and it ripped her chest in two. She'd meant it in the teasing, joking way they usually had, but given how everyone else talked about him, he could take it very differently. Instead of stepping back, away from her, he pressed in closer, his body taking up her entire field of vision, his storm cloud expression inches from her.

"Kissing you will be nothing like kissing them."

The words were a knife in her wildly beating heart, stopping it short. If she was going to be mean, then so was he, it seemed. She tilted her head up, blinking away the moisture in her eyes. "Because I don't know how?"

A hand slid up to cup the back of her neck and he leaned in close, his breath a tickle on her cheek. "Because I'm not doing it to forget, but to make you forget."

Before she could even think about asking him what he meant, his lips were there, hovering over hers, his breath hot on her mouth. His other hand was on her waist, and if not for that and the wall behind her digging into her spine, she was sure she'd be on the floor. Her knees had stopped supporting her ages ago.

Clementine waited for Austin to make the final push, to bring their lips together, but he held off, waiting. The beat of his heart was thumping against her chest, and the smell of his skin invaded her nose. There was no heavy cologne, just the clean, soapy mintiness she'd never noticed until now. Now that they were pressed together against her wall about to do the one thing she'd been thinking about since she met him years ago.

When she realized he was waiting for her to do it, for her to take control of her first kiss, she melted completely into him.

It was unlike anything she could have imagined. His mouth was soft, so soft, and yet hard as steel. The press of him was a thousand stars fluttering across her skin, twinkling and electric. His hands were wrapped around her, his fingers clinging to her like he never wanted to let go. And she didn't want him to. Not ever.

He pulled back slightly and she took a breath, her lips parting for just a moment. Then he dove in, exploring gently with his tongue, and her world exploded beneath her closed eyelids. She was trembling, not sure how she was still standing while the earth spun beneath her.

Wrapping her hands around his neck, she pulled him tighter to her, breathing him in in big gulps, gasping for more of him, like she was drowning in the ocean and he was the sky.

Nothing her friends had said over the years compared to this. No one had ever told her it would be like dissolving into another person so completely. Fire licked at her nerves, from her toes to her eyelashes. Everything burned, hotter than mid-July pavement.

Finally, after years had gone by, Austin pulled away again and leaned his forehead on hers and stayed away. He was breathing heavily, his irises nearly black. When he lifted his head to look in her eyes, he licked his lips, bright red from their kiss. The world was still spinning for Clementine, but at least she had the wall at her back to support her. Austin had nothing to lean on and looked like he was about to float away.

Neither of them said anything for several long minutes, both breathing heavy, their arms still wrapped around each other. The longer he was quiet, the more anxiety wrapped itself around her chest, squeezing tight.

Maybe... it hadn't been that great for him. Maybe he didn't know how to tell her it wasn't supposed to ignite like that. She was too eager, too full of years of pent-up desire. For Austin, for Mark, for the countless other crushes she'd never had the guts to talk to the way she wanted. The only reason she'd been able to let go like that was because this was just practice. It didn't matter what Austin thought, it didn't matter if he hadn't liked the kiss. This wasn't something real.

Right?

"So... was I okay?" she finally asked, the wall hard and unforgiving at her back. She shifted to relieve the pressure, her heart beating wildly while waiting for his answer. Better to know than to die a thousand deaths waiting for him to say anything.

"That was..." Austin took a step back, his arms finally dropping from Clementine's shoulders, and shook his head. Her stomach dropped. "Are you sure you've never kissed anyone before?"

The air that had been heavy around her just a moment before lightened in an instant. A relieved giggle burst out of her. "I mean, I did kiss Matt Hayes on the cheek once."

A muscle twitched in Austin's jaw. "When was this? Does Dani know about this?"

She stifled another giggle. Of course he'd noticed the unspoken thing between her sister and the Floodline's bartender.

"Fourth grade. He told me I had cooties. Clementine Cootie was my nickname for years."

"I'll have to talk to him about that."

Now she laughed, his expression so serious it had to be a joke. "I don't think it's entirely his fault I never kissed anyone. It was partly Bastien being so intimidating, partly being Dr. Miller's kid, and partly my own shyness."

"You're not shy anymore."

"Well, not around my fake boyfriend, no." She grinned at him, letting him know she didn't mind making fun of herself. How could she, now that she'd finally had the first kiss to end all first kisses, and she knew he'd liked it too? "And you've mostly seen me around my family. I'm more comfortable around them."

Except she wasn't, not like she used to be. Not since she went for the DPT rather than MD route. Not since she felt that distance that had always existed between her and the rest of her family widen, almost imperceptibly at first, until now it felt like a gaping valley with her on one side and the rest of them on the other. It wasn't that she minded the gap exactly, but she'd always been a bit lonely.

It was nice to have someone on her side of the valley. Even if it was temporary. Even if it was pretend.

He took a step back and crossed his arms, his piercing eyes looking her up and down. "You're not comfortable around them though. Not really, are you?"

She sucked in a breath. Perceptive as usual, Austin had figured out her secret. Though he didn't know everything, she reminded herself. He hadn't known she'd never been kissed.

"It's been getting better. Having a boyfriend, even a fake one, has been helping."

He tucked a strand of her hair behind her ear, his face as perfect and cool as a Greek sculpture. "Well, I'm happy to help."

"I just wish I could help you more than I am."

Marbles meowed from behind them. It was almost dinnertime. Austin's eyes flicked away for a second, before coming back to focus on her. "Trust me, you are."

And she knew, just like Austin always seemed to know, that he wasn't talking about his shoulder or the skiing.

"What was the question you wanted to ask me earlier?" she asked while her cat nudged at her leg, looking for food.

"Hmm?" Austin's attention was on the cat again. "Oh, I don't remember."

This time, Clementine knew he was lying.

Austin hadn't been able to do his full cleaning routine with his shoulder in a sling, which, more than anything else about the injury, had unsettled him. Two days after taking off his sling and one day after his PT-slash-make-out session with Clementine, he was going over everything in his kitchen twice with the dedication and precision that only came over him when he was trying to distract himself from something.

That something was Clementine Miller.

Every woman he'd been with after Cassidy had served one purpose only: distracting him from his pain and loneliness. Most had done the job well, some had even been unexpectedly diverting, but never enough so that he remembered any details about them for more than a few weeks.

As he wiped down the counter next to his sink with smooth and practiced strokes, he knew that his kiss with Clementine would be burned into his memory for the rest of his life.

Nothing had ever felt so right, and the only thing stopping him from driving straight over to her house to tell her was the fact that it had all been practice for her. He'd wanted to make her forget about Mark, forget about anything other than him, but of course, that hadn't worked. She'd called him her fake boyfriend not even two minutes after that kiss, so if that's really all she wanted from him, that's what he'd keep doing. It's why he hadn't asked her the question he'd been thinking about since his conversation with Anais: did she want to try dating for real?

But holy hell, that kiss had been something else.

Just as he was cutting up a lemon to put in a bowl of water to clean his oven, there was a knock at his door.

It was Clementine.

"I don't remember scheduling a house call." He grinned, too pleased to see her to hide it, especially when he noticed she was still in her uniform from the PT clinic. The olive-green shirt with "Vickers Physical Therapy" written above the pocket was the wrong color for her, but she looked great.

He couldn't help but hope that something had changed. She'd come straight from work to see him. Maybe the kiss hadn't been practice for her after all. Maybe she felt something more, the same something that had been brewing inside of him since they started this ridiculous farce.

Not that he'd ever admit that to her.

"I just did something really stupid."

She brushed past him, into his entry hall, clueless that her words had sent his heart shooting into his throat. There were only a few possibilities here.

She'd told Mark how she felt about him.

Or, thanks to the confidence from Austin's spontaneous lesson, she'd kissed Mark.

Both options made him want to punch something, but luckily, he remembered just in time that despite being mostly healed, his shoulder was in no shape for that kind of outward display of anger.

"And you need help?"

"Of course. That's why I came here." She flopped onto his couch and put her hands over her face.

This soothed his raging jealousy a fraction. She could have

gone to her sister or Gabby or one of her friends. She'd come to him.

He settled in the chair across from her, using all of his control to keep a giant grin off his face. Instead, he schooled his features into the serious, considerate expression he used with patients. "How can I help?"

"I may have said we'd bring dessert for Thanksgiving."

Once again, Clementine Miller surprised him. His lips curved up. "That wasn't what I was expecting you to say."

"I'm a terrible cook."

"Now that can't possibly be true."

She groaned and covered her face with her hands. "It's not my fault. Dad made everything, so I never had to learn. I lived off dried ramen and takeout in school. He would be horrified."

"Ah, so your family doesn't know you don't cook."

This was getting better and better. Would she ever stop being so fascinating? He hoped not. He wanted to discover new things about Clementine Miller forever.

Then he remembered she wouldn't be his forever.

"Will you help me, Austin?" She removed her hands from her face to stare at him with wide, pleading-puppy brown eyes. His chest squeezed tight and his throat went dry.

"What makes you think I'm any good at cooking?"

"Because you're good at everything."

"If that were true, I wouldn't be single right now."

"You're not."

His heart swelled at the possibility behind those words.

Her cheeks flushed. "I mean, yes, you are technically single. I'm just your fake girlfriend."

"Are you?" The words left his mouth before his normally logical brain could stop him. They seemed to have the same effect on Clementine as they did on him: complete and total shock. The rigid planes of her face were unreadable. All he could see was the heat he'd put there from his kiss that he wanted to put there again as often as possible.

He cleared his throat. "I mean, you're not just my fake girlfriend. We're friends."

She looked down, disappointment coloring her features for the briefest moment before her lips turned up in a familiar, wicked smile. "Only if you help me with this. Or I'll tell your whole family when I meet them what a bad kisser you are."

"Blackmailing me into friendship? You're even more devious than I thought you were. That's something I would do."

She beamed up at him. "Coming from you, there's no higher compliment."

There were lots of other ways he wanted to compliment her, but it fell under neither the friend nor fake-girlfriend category, at least not when they were alone. He'd already gotten himself into enough of an emotional mess with his brilliant kissing lesson idea.

"What do you want to make?"

He led her into his kitchen and tucked away the bowl of lemons in a corner of the counter, the gleaming tile reflecting the soft overhead lighting. The oven could wait. Night came early during the winter in Jasper Creek, and for Austin, there was nothing cozier than cooking. Though it had been years since he'd done it with a partner.

She brushed past him, his skin burning where their bodies had touched. He closed his eyes briefly to savor it, then opened them to find her sticking her head into his fridge.

"This is the most organized refrigerator I have ever seen in my life."

"I'd say thank you, but I don't think you mean it as a compliment."

"Of course I do. Everything about you deserves a compliment."

Austin didn't think Clementine fully realized what she was doing to him. If she did, she would likely use it against him. He wasn't sure what he wanted more right now.

"Why don't we make a pecan pie? I know all the Millers like that."

"I don't."

"Really?" His eyebrows shot up. "How have I never noticed that?"

She shrugged and looked away. "I'll eat it if it's there, and everyone else likes it, so I don't complain."

This was the old Clementine. His chest swelled, not quite knowing what he wanted to do.

"So what do you like?"

"Chocolate mousse." No hesitation at all. She knew what she wanted but still wasn't fully able to say it to her family. Or even to him, unless he asked.

"Well then, let's make chocolate mousse."

"Now?"

"Do you have somewhere else to be?" His tone was teasing, but his chest squeezed tight. Maybe she was moving things into the friend zone because something had happened with Mark. Maybe someone else had noticed this amazing woman.

"Do you?" Her lips curled up, and he laughed, the tension leaving his body in a rush of endorphins.

"Touché, Miller."

With his direction, she got out all the ingredients and bowls, commenting, of course, on the organization of his cabinets as well. Seeing her moving around his space was doing odd things to his stomach. He had to grip the edge of the counter to stop himself from wrapping her in his arms and asking her to stay forever.

"I can't be the only one to have said something about your kitchen." She pulled out a knife from the block, sharp and gleaming as if it were new thanks to his regular sharpening routine.

"You're the only one who's seen it."

"What? Really?" She looked around. "You've never cooked for anyone, had friends over?"

"I see Matt and Carter at the Floodline. Anais and Gabby at

work or their houses." He shifted against the counter he was leaning on, knowing she'd follow up if he didn't answer the first part of her question as well. "I haven't cooked for anyone since I lived in Denver."

"Where your only significant ex lives, not caring or knowing where you live now."

He sucked in a breath. Of course she'd remember his words. It didn't mean anything other than she was just as smart and observant as he always knew she was.

"What happened?" she said, putting two bowls next to each other, then stacking them up again.

"With what?"

She bit her lip, and he didn't make her say it. He knew exactly what she wanted, what she deserved to know. She'd trusted him enormously up to this point, revealing things no one else knew about her, and he should be able to do the same.

He took a deep breath. "The simple answer is she cheated on me."

The shock was predictable, but he was still immensely satisfied to see it. There'd been whispers at the hospital that it was what he deserved, that someone so smart and attractive couldn't have all the luck. But for those who knew him—for someone like Clementine who still thought the world of him and didn't think his hyperorganized kitchen was weird or his know-it-all tendencies irritating—of course she'd be baffled that anyone would willingly give him up.

"I knew about it but didn't call it out for months. I was in the middle of my fellowship, and I thought it would work itself out."

"Because you can be very stupid when you're in love."

He smiled. Had she memorized everything he'd ever said to her? It would be only fitting since he'd done the same.

"The more complicated answer involves my family." When she opened her mouth to ask what he knew she would, he held up a hand. "I don't want to say much more since you'll be meeting them soon. I don't want you to go in with my opinions of them in your head."

She frowned at this. "Are they not nice people?"

"They're wonderful. I love them a lot. I miss them a lot."

The frown deepened, her dark eyes a riot of beautiful confusion. "But you live here, not California."

"Like I said, it's complicated." He smiled and opened a cabinet to pull out a few bars of baking chocolate. "But I'm sure you'll figure it out quickly, once we're there."

He let this sink in for a few minutes while he gathered the rest of what they'd need for the recipe, waiting to see if she'd have more questions. Finally, when she'd remained silent long enough, he gestured at the ingredients spread across his counter.

"Should we get started? The cream will go bad if it stays out much longer."

At this, she shook herself, then rolled her eyes. "It takes at least two hours."

He smiled. "Do I want to know how you know that?"

There was a slight tinge to her cheeks, but her smile was the wicked one he was growing addicted to. "No. And don't ever mention bad milk to Eli."

His laugh echoed off the kitchen walls, and she snickered along with him. It was exactly how he'd pictured spending nights in his kitchen. Laughing with someone, talking and having fun.

Maybe it wouldn't be totally impossible. After all, she hadn't mentioned Mark once all night.

"First step: cut the chocolate."

She nodded, her eyes determined. The knife was wobbly in her hand, however, and he came up behind her to steady it. Putting his other hand on top of the chocolate she was trying to chop, he guided her movements, showing her how to angle the knife so it didn't scatter when she cut into it.

The warmth of her body melted into him, her hands loose and

trusting beneath his. He breathed in deeply, her hair brushing against his cheek as he leaned into her further.

Suddenly, she dropped the knife and spun around. Her eyes bore into his, searching for he wasn't sure what, but his heart pounded in his head, hoping that she wanted the same thing he did.

"Can I kiss you again?"

The floor fell out from under his feet, and his heart sang to hear the request he'd been hoping for since she burst into his house tonight. When would she stop surprising him? He put his hands on the counter, trapping her between his body and the counter.

"Now why would you want to do that?"

Her throat contracted as she swallowed, but her eyes never left his.

"I think I need more practice."

The blood drained from his brain so fast he was dizzy. "Practice? Expecting to need it soon?"

There was a flash of something in her eyes at the reminder of who and what this was all for, but she shook her head, and he couldn't quite catch the emotions there. "I just want to. Is that okay?"

"More than okay." The words came out in a strangle of sound.

A beat passed, then another, and they stared into each other's hungry eyes. Then she grabbed his neck and pulled him to her, and he forgot about his jealousy. He forgot about everything other than her. The heat of her body against his, the slide of her lips on his mouth, the soft sighs she let out that only he would ever hear.

When they pulled out of the kiss, they were both breathing heavily, and her eyes were shiny with desire. The urge to pull her in again was so strong he knew if he did, they'd never come up again. And that wasn't the plan. He had to remember the plan, or risk losing himself completely and ending up heartbroken when yet another woman chose someone else over him. It had happened too often for this to end any other way, no matter how incredible their kisses were.

He took a step back and smiled, brushing her hair back from her face. "You should do what you want more often."

"With you, I feel like I can."

Even if this was all for Mark, she also wanted Austin. It was etched into every line of her face, every tilt of her eyebrows and the curve of her lips.

He knew it as well as he knew where every single item in his refrigerator was.

But he'd been wrong before.

It didn't feel real. Clementine had kissed Austin again, and he didn't seem to mind. In fact, he seemed to like it even more than the first time.

Looking around the mess in the kitchen, she was reminded of the real reason she'd come here. "We should finish the mousse."

"It's almost done." He played with the ends of her hair, dragging his fingers along her collarbone in a very distracting way. "We just need to fold in the egg whites, then it needs to set."

"For how long?"

"A few hours to overnight."

Disappointment rippled through her, and she took a step back out of reach of his hands. She should go, let him get on with his evening, and come back tomorrow.

Or she could be bold. "Should we play a puzzle while we wait? I kind of want to taste the mousse to make sure you haven't tricked me into making something terrible."

There was a deep rumble in his chest that made her entire body light up.

"If anyone's been tricked, I'd say it was me."

Heat spread through her, and she looked around the kitchen

again. There were bowls and utensils everywhere, streaks of melted chocolate on counters. The pristine space was a wreck, and it was all her fault. She put an egg-covered whisk back into the bowl they'd used to beat the whites into fluffy white peaks. "What do you mean?"

He slid next to her, his body pressing gently into her side, and picked up a spatula. "I thought you said you didn't know how to cook."

"I don't." She watched the hypnotic rhythm of his hands as they folded the egg whites into the melted chocolate.

"So what am I doing right now?"

"Folding in egg whites."

He glanced at her, eyebrow raised, as if proving his point.

She picked up the empty bowl full of utensils and carried it over to the sink. "Just because I know the terminology doesn't mean I'm any good at it." She doused a sponge with soap and got to work cleaning. "I know the difference between an otoscope and an ophthalmoscope, but that doesn't mean I'd make a good doctor."

He stopped folding in the eggs and set the bowl down on the counter. "Is that why you went to PT school? You thought you'd make a bad doctor?"

"No, that's not why." She bit her lip and rinsed out the bowl again, even though it was as clean as any dish ever could be.

Austin didn't say anything, and she knew he was waiting for an answer. If she wanted this thing with him to be real, then she'd have to be real. Gathering her courage, she set the clean bowl aside and leaned against the sink.

"I haven't wanted to be a doctor for a long time." She glanced at him to gauge his reaction. His face was intensely beautiful and entirely focused on her. Her heart gave a stutter and she gripped the edge of the sink. "I never pictured spending my entire life in Jasper Creek. If I were a doctor, then I'd be part of the family busi-ness and I'd never do anything on my own. Does that sound terrible?"

There was the flicker of a smile on the lips she'd just been kissing not ten minutes earlier. "It sounds very familiar, Cutie. I can relate."

"Can you?" She crossed her arms and tilted her head to one side. "What does your family do? I guess I just assumed they're doctors."

"And you know what they say about assumptions." In one single, smooth movement, he picked up the bowl and put it in the fridge. "Now, I believe you mentioned wanting to work on a puzzle while we wait to taste my mousse and prove you can trust me and my cooking advice."

"I do trust you, Dino."

His hand stilled on the fridge door, and she had a pang in her chest to think it might not have been the right time for the ridiculous nickname. She wanted to keep talking to him. She liked talking to him. She liked him. A lot.

Clementine made her way over to him and took his hand in hers. Only then did he look at her, his eyes blazing. "I trusted you with my first kiss. I can't imagine kissing anyone else will be like that."

"It won't be." Austin drew a hand up to her cheek and then back through her hair. She closed her eyes briefly, savoring the feel of his skin on hers. "I'm the best kisser you'll ever know."

She snort-laughed, and her eyes flew open at the unattractive sound, horror spiking in her chest. There was no look of disgust on his face, no smirk at the noise, only his eyes on hers, looking like he wanted to eat her alive.

"Should we try to do this for real?" Her voice was so soft, so scared, but at least she'd said the words out loud. Something about Austin made her bold at the same time it made her nervous.

"What?" There was the barest flicker of surprise in his eyes, then his face slipped into a mask that was impossible to read, a beautiful carved marble statue. "What about Mark?"

Clementine wrinkled her nose. What could she say that wasn't a lie but wasn't admitting just how right Austin had been? "He… might not be who I thought he was."

A smirk flittered on the edges of his mouth. "You mean he's an annoying prick? I think I told you that."

Despite her nerves, she bit her lip to stop from laughing. Austin leaned forward to tug at her chin. She loved when he did this. This tiny bit of contact sent electricity through her, making her skin tingle and stomach swirl.

"Austin, you're making this harder than it needs to be."

He was still standing right in front of her, his hand gently running through her hair. "I just want to understand what you want."

It was hard to concentrate with his fingers in her hair, but she took a deep breath and powered through it. "I want to not be practicing all the time. If it's not going to be Mark, then it'll be someone, someday. I want to know what it's like to really go out with a guy and not be calculating if we're at the right angle or what to do to make people look at us. I just want to try it for real."

His eyes were fixed on hers, and though she couldn't read any particular change in his expression, she could feel a hesitancy in him like he was holding his breath, bracing for some kind of impact.

Her stomach dropped and she stepped back, his hand finally releasing her hair. "It's okay if you don't want to. I just thought that we were getting along so well—"

"Of course I want to date you for real, Cutie. You're incredible."

The world tilted on its axis and the breath left her body. She stumbled back into the counter, and he caught her arms to hold her upright, a small upward tilt to his lips.

"Why don't we keep the same end date? That way there's no pressure around breaking up once you get tired of me."

Tired of him? All she wanted was to be with him all the time. But of course he might not feel the same. Dating wasn't a promise of marriage, after all. It was trying someone out, seeing how you fit together. "I won't get tired of you."

"You haven't seen me with my family." He chuckled and shook his head. "You'll be able to put up with me better knowing it'll end anyway once we're back from skiing."

Clementine didn't like this idea at all, but he did have a point. Dating someone like Austin—really dating him—would be a lot for her, as inexperienced as she was. It might not go the way she imagined, and then the thought of having to break up with him without knowing how seemed impossible. Though it also seemed impossible that she'd ever want to break up with him, but what did she know? This was her first relationship ever. Maybe he would annoy her after a while.

"Okay, deal. We're a real couple until we get off the plane from California."

The smile that spread across his face was so dazzling, she wasn't sure how she'd ever get used to it. But then she remembered with a twinge in her chest that she'd only have until New Year's, then it wouldn't be hers at all.

Austin knocked on Clementine's door on Thanksgiving morning, his heart hammering and his palms sweating. To the outside world, nothing had changed, and yet everything was different.

It had been a week, and they'd talked every night on the phone like a real couple would. They'd been to the Floodline again. This time Matt had joined them for a drink, and it had been... perfect. Real. Something had shifted, and though it was still fragile, it could still all fall apart, Austin hadn't been this hopeful in years.

But not quite hopeful enough to admit just how deep he was feeling things to Clementine. Just in case. She still had his family to meet, after all. That was always the beginning of the end for his relationships. Why would this one be any different? The solid end date kept things safe, gave them both a way out that would be less painful than the monthslong saga that it had been with Cassidy. It was the smart thing to do, and intelligent woman that she was, Clementine had agreed.

There was a loud meow from behind the door, and Clementine's voice chastised her cat.

"No, you've had enough bacon. I need to go."

When she opened the door, he was smiling widely, the peek at her domestic life pleasing him more than he realized. Making chocolate mousse together was one thing, but to share a life with someone like Clementine Miller would be more than he deserved. He'd have to content himself with sharing a few holidays with her.

"Hi." There was a shyness to her tone that hadn't been there in years. Her eyes didn't quite meet his, and her bottom lip was under her teeth in that all-too-familiar hesitancy he'd been working so hard to get rid of. But maybe this was a different kind of hesitancy. The fluttery, jittery kind he also had inklings of as he thought about spending a major holiday with a woman and her family for the first time in over three years.

"Hey." He leaned forward and tugged at her chin, releasing her bottom lip from the bite of her teeth. It took an enormous amount of self-control not to kiss her. "You look amazing."

Her hair was in soft curls, and she had on more makeup than her usual swipe of mascara and lip gloss. The deep green dress was the perfect color, and her skin was glowing, except where it was pink with a blush at his words.

"Thanks. I figured they'd expect me to dress nicer if I'm bringing a boyfriend."

There was the subtlest of lies in her words. She didn't care about her family, she wanted to look nice for him. His heart expanded in his chest. He'd worn a tie, just for her, though if she asked, he'd also say it was for the benefit of her family.

"So it's all for them?"

She nodded, then her eyes met his, and she stood up a little straighter, their game of emotional chicken giving her the strength he knew it would. "Yes, just for them. For show."

"Well, it's a lovely show."

They walked to the car, the unspoken realization that they both knew she was lying floating heavily in the air between them.

"What do you usually do for Thanksgiving?" Clementine asked when they were settled in the car for the short drive to her parents' house.

"I go skiing." Which he wouldn't have been able to do anyway this year with his shoulder still healing.

"With your family?"

He shook his head and turned onto the main street in Jasper Creek. "I see them enough during the Christmas trip."

"But I thought you missed them?"

"I do. It's just not worth the flight and drive for only a few days."

"How very logical."

He grinned at this and cast a sideways glance at her. "They get it. They're like me."

"Are they all doctors?"

"Why so many questions all of a sudden?"

Her face was pulled into a thoughtful expression, eyes crinkled, like she was trying to figure something out.

"I just... figured I should know all of this in case someone asks today. It would be weird if I didn't know what you usually do for the holidays."

"If you don't know something, just tell them we're too busy making out to do much talking."

"Austin!" It was exactly the kind of scandalized reaction he'd been hoping to get. Her face was beet red and she shifted in her seat. "I can't say that to them. It's not even true."

"Only if you don't want it to be." The words spilled from him before he could consider them.

"Really?"

They were on her parents' street, and he pulled alongside the curb in front of the house. Her eyes were on him, her question hanging in the air between them, eagerness and desire flitting across her face.

"We can turn around right now and spend the day just the two of us." He knew she'd say no, but he wanted her to know it was a possibility.

There was already so much that Clementine had done to forge

her own path, to come out of her shell, and Austin knew she could do more.

If she wanted it.

She bit her lip and met his eyes, asking wordlessly what he wanted to do. He tugged at her chin and her mouth popped open, a question already forming there.

"But today, the most important thing is that your family likes me. So we should probably go inside."

She made a face, scrunching up her nose and pouting. "They're really getting on my nerves lately."

This surprised him, though it shouldn't at this point with Clementine. He wanted to ask her more about how she didn't want to live in Jasper Creek forever, what she pictured for her life long-term, what family meant to her... but sitting in the car in front of her parents' house was not the appropriate moment to delve into it.

"If you want to leave early, just say *puppy*."

Her lips turned up. "And if you want to leave, just say Marbles."

She got out of the car, and he followed her, laughing the entire way to the door.

The day was loud and chaotic. With Eli and Dani home from school and both clamoring for time with baby Jamie, both Gabby and Bastien got the break they desperately needed. They spent most of the morning snoozing in front of the parade on TV while people wandered in and out, bringing mixing bowls and trays of snacks and toys for Jamie.

There was too much food and stories about past Thanksgivings and teasing and name calling and too much wine. It reminded him of being with his family.

It was perfect.

Midway through the afternoon, after turkey but before dessert,

Anais stood up at the crowded dining room table, beaming. "We have some news."

Clementine and Gabby looked over at Austin, identical knowing expressions on their faces. Thanks to his keen observational skills, they already knew what was coming. Though they would, of course, act surprised at the official announcement Anais was about to make.

"There'll be another little Miller here with us next Thanksgiving."

The two oldest Miller doctors cried out, clapping their hands and standing up to hug Anais and Jackson.

Mouth agape, Bastien turned to his wife. "Gabby, did you know about this?"

"Austin predicted this last month at the Fall Festival. You were there when he said it."

"I thought he was joking," Bastien grumbled, a sour look on his face.

Clementine and Austin snickered, along with Dani and Eli, but Anais was glaring at Austin, looking less than amused.

Gabby rolled her eyes and ignored Bastien to smile up at Anais while Jamie bounced happily on her knees. "Congratulations. Jamie needs a little playmate, and it won't be a brother or sister anytime soon."

"Is he still not sleeping?" The Miller matriarch frowned and turned to Gabby, launching into a series of questions, while Dani and Eli chatted happily with Anais. On the other side of Gabby, Jackson and Bastien were grinning and talking about their plans for total Miller domination of Jasper Creek's youth sports leagues.

The atmosphere was so joyful it took Austin a minute to notice the stillness hidden behind Clementine's smile.

"Are you okay?" he whispered in her ear, and she turned to him.

Their faces were so close he could kiss her if he wanted to. He did want to, he always wanted to, but this wasn't the right moment.

"I'm fine." Her eyes were on her plate, the lie of her words etched inside them. "Are you okay? This puts a lot of pressure on you."

"Me? Why?" He looked around the table.

Everyone was still focused on Anais and Jackson, Bastien now giving her advice, Gabby giving actually useful advice, and her parents listing all the early pregnancy precautions to follow, as if they'd forgotten in the five minutes since she announced it that their daughter was a fully certified and capable doctor in her own right.

"I'll be next." Her voice was low, her words a hot breath on his cheek. "To get married, have kids. You're here at Thanksgiving this year, so they're already thinking it will be you."

It was all too easy for him to think the same thing. He had been thinking the same thing, but to hear how clearly she didn't want that was enough to banish the thought from his mind and bring on the shame of even thinking it in the first place.

"You're only twenty-five. Nobody's expecting that from you."

"My mom had twins by my age. And had started her residency."

"Since when does Clementine Miller do anything like the rest of her family?"

Her lips turned up at this, and he almost kissed her right there. She was so beautiful.

"Austin?" From the other side of the table, Anais was looking at him expectantly. "Can you help me grab some glasses?"

With a squeeze of Clementine's hand, he stood, leaving her still looking a little shell-shocked.

In the kitchen, Austin was able to give Anais the hug he'd been dying to for the past few months but couldn't since she stubbornly refused to either tell people or admit it to herself.

"You know I've known for months?"

"Of course you did. You also know why I was so upset about you and Clementine."

"I don't, actually."

She raised her eyebrows. "Really? I think that's only the second time I've ever heard you say you don't know something."

He rolled his eyes at her. "That attending was lying. There's no way that clavicle could have been broken, it was crystal clear in the X-ray."

Anais giggled at the familiar banter they'd shared through residency and his first years working with her in Jasper Creek. Then her lips pursed, her expression serious again. "Austin, come on, you can't expect me to be thrilled about the possibility of you leaving."

"And where exactly am I going?"

She reached up into a cabinet above the sink, pulled out a set of champagne glasses, and put them next to the bottle of fizzy apple juice out on the counter. "Your last bad breakup led you here to Jasper Creek. What happens when you break Minnie's heart? You'll leave."

The words sank in, each one a heavy weight on Austin's shoulders. He could tell her. Anais was no stranger to secrets, her own relationship with Jackson having started as a secret summer fling. But it wasn't his secret to tell. And he liked it too much that they all thought this had started as something real. That Clementine would actually want to be with someone like him.

"It's much more likely she'll break mine, you know."

"Minnie? A heartbreaker?" Anais shook her head. "That's not the Clementine I know."

"She's not the same person she was before she left for school."

"I know that."

"Do you?"

At this, Anais hesitated, her eyes casting around, as if looking for answers in the pictures of the Millers scattered around the kitchen. The bulletin board on the back of the door to the basement was full of them, the refrigerator was covered with snapshots of Jamie, more than probably even Bastien and Gabby had. Anais saw who her sister had been. Austin knew who she was now.

"Well, whatever the case, I only see this ending one way, and that's with you leaving. And I don't want you to."

"The only way you see it ending?" A muscle tightened in Austin's jaw. "And what if this is it? For both of us? Would it be that bad to have me as a brother-in-law?"

Anais paled, and the reality of what he'd just said hit him right in the middle of the chest. It was completely ridiculous that barely a month into a relationship, he was talking about marriage. Meanwhile, Clementine seemed terrified of the expectation that she'd be the next Miller sibling to enter that phase of her life.

Good thing the relationship was ending in a few weeks, no matter what.

And yet the image of Clementine on his arm, saying words Austin never imagined he would, was all too easy for his brain to provide him.

"It would be wonderful," Anais whispered, tears pooling in the corner of her eyes. "I guess you'll just have to prove me wrong."

"Will you admit you're wrong?"

"Never." Her lips twitched, her eyes still moist. "But you'll be allowed exactly one 'I told you so.'"

He knew he'd never need to use it, but he hugged her, and by the time he pulled back, her eyes were dry.

"Ready for dessert?"

"Always."

Once they were both back at the table, the conversation was on the differences between Thanksgiving dishes across the country. Heather Miller hadn't grown up in Colorado, and Jackson was from South Carolina, so they were sharing what their families would make for the holiday. Austin put his hand on Clementine's and let his attention wander.

"You'll come help, won't you, Gibson?" Bastien looked over at Austin, and it took Austin a confused second to refocus on the conversation. His mind had been back in the kitchen with Anais, going over what she'd said.

"Help?"

"The Winter Festival. I need to start setting up next weekend."

He realized now it wasn't actually a question. This was what would be expected of him, of someone Clementine dated. It was a sign that Bastien was taking this seriously, to be including him in something only available to family.

Austin was touched. Something in his chest shifted, an unexpected emotion getting caught somewhere between his stomach and his throat.

"Of course."

Bastien nodded once, an approving look on his face. Beside him, Gabby beamed.

Then Clementine squeezed his hand. "Bastien, don't make Austin do something he may not have time for."

She caught his eye and understanding washed over him. She was giving him an out. Already thinking ahead to next year, when they wouldn't be together, not wanting to commit him to something he wouldn't want to do again. Or wouldn't be around to do.

"I'm happy to help." It would help with Bastien and Anais. Both of them were worried, for different reasons, but this was a way to show them how serious he was.

Maybe Clementine would finally catch on.

Getting married and having kids of her own might be the last thing on Clementine's mind, but she loved being an aunt. She offered to watch Jamie while Bastien set up the Winter Festival and Gabby had a morning to herself.

Of course, Jamie immediately started crying the second his parents were out of the house. The only thing that seemed to keep him calm was walking. The calm, easy day she'd pictured sitting curled up on the couch with a mug of hot chocolate while he rolled around then napped disappeared within minutes of arriving at their house.

Rather than pace around the living room, she strapped him to her chest, covered him up, and headed out into the winter morning. After a half hour of tromping through the snow while Jamie babbled happily, she arrived at the park next to Town Square. She could see Austin helping Bastien with lights along the fence across the street. The festival wouldn't open for another few hours, and she knew they'd been there since dawn setting things up. For Bastien to ask Austin for help was huge. It was a sign her brother had finally accepted the idea of her dating him.

Just in time for them to break up in a few weeks.

What if we didn't?

The thought came out of nowhere, yet it wasn't the first time she'd had it. The shift had been so slow she didn't know when exactly it had happened. Maybe the kiss—kisses, she remembered with a shiver that had nothing to do with the cold. Maybe Thanksgiving, having him next to her supporting her in that subtle, deep way he seemed to instinctively know how to do.

But the shift on her side didn't mean anything had changed for Austin. He'd been the one to push for things to end after their trip to California. The trip she still hadn't mentioned to her family.

The Millers always celebrated the holidays together. Even if Clementine tried hard to distinguish herself from the rest of her family, even if she dreamed of living somewhere else, she truly did love spending time with them. Just not all of her time.

As she tramped through the snow, she cuddled Jamie closer to her and gave him a little kiss on top of the head. She got a happy snuffle in return and her heart doubled in size.

When she'd agreed to go with Austin to California as part of their fake-dating deal, it had seemed so far off. Now, a little over a week before they were set to leave, she still hadn't figured out how to tell her family that for the first time in decades, Christmas would be missing one of the Miller household. This hadn't been an issue for Jackson or Gabby, who both had no contact with their own families. Clementine would be the first Miller sibling to celebrate the holiday with their significant other. Normally she liked doing her own thing, but this felt consequential in a very different way than choosing physical therapy over general medicine.

"What do you think, Jamie?" she whispered to her nephew. "Will they be mad at me or happy for me?"

Jamie blew a raspberry. She sighed and kept up her circle around the park, as she watched Austin put up lights along Main Street with her brother. Clementine was across the street at the park, bouncing on her half-frozen feet to keep Jamie happy. It was hard to tell from this distance if her brother and her no-longer-fake boyfriend were getting along, or even talking, but at least they seemed to be working together well enough.

As if he could tell his aunt was not giving her full attention to him, Jamie started fussing. She set off again, taking a long, wandering path that would eventually lead to where the two men were working.

They didn't seem to notice her approaching since they were so focused on their work. It was easy in the quiet morning for her to hear their conversation, even as far away as she was.

"You've been a big help today, Austin," Bastien said, his eyes still on the lights in his hand.

The use of his first name was notable, but Austin didn't sound affected by it. He'd probably known it was coming. "Thanks."

"I don't ask a lot of people for help, so you do realize how special you are?"

"I've always known how special I am, even without you telling me, Bastien."

The groan her brother let out sounded so much like Anais, Clementine bit back a giggle. "You realize it's because you say things like that that people want to punch you in the face?"

"Nobody wants to punch me in the face except you, I think."

"Gee, I wonder why?"

The path she was on wound around a few trees, and from where she was standing, they couldn't see her. But she could see them perfectly. Austin put down the strand of lights he was holding to cross his arms.

"I'm not sure I know what you mean."

"If you break her heart, you know I'm legally obligated to kill you, right?"

"Why does everyone seem to think I'll be the one to do the breaking?" Austin sighed and shook his head.

Clementine stopped in her tracks, heart hammering. What on earth did he mean by that?

He's probably just setting the foundation for the breakup that's coming after our trip.

The trip that Bastien didn't know about yet.

"She's just a kid. I don't want her to get hurt."

"She's twenty-five, Bastien, and perfectly capable of making her own decisions. She chose to be with me. She knew exactly what she was getting into."

Bastien pursed his lips, his eyes looking away from Austin. The frantic pattern of Clementine's heartbeat didn't slow down in the least.

"She's smart and funny and determined to get what she wants."

Clementine leaned against the snow-covered tree next to her and inhaled slowly through her nose. Austin's words weren't doing anything to slow down her pulse.

"I know."

"No, you don't. If you did, then you'd trust her to know what she wants and to get it no matter what. She's just like her big brother and sister in that way."

"You're talking about her being a PT."

"Among other things."

Clementine's stomach clenched. He meant Mark, of course. Even if he wasn't what she wanted anymore, that's how this whole thing with Austin had started.

She hadn't thought of it that way before, that she was like Bastien and Anais. They'd always seemed so much more certain and confident. Being different from her siblings had meant she felt less than. But maybe she wasn't that different after all.

"I do trust her, I just..." Bastien looked away. "I just want her to be happy. And if that's with you, then I can live with that."

"If you wanted her to be happy, you wouldn't be policing the decisions of a grown woman. She's terrified of disappointing you and Anais. Do you know that?"

The conflict on Bastien's face was clear, even from a distance.

Of course he knew. They were all brilliant, the Millers, but that didn't mean they always acted as logically and sensibly as Austin did.

Well, as he usually did. Ranting at his not-so-fake girlfriend's brother wasn't very high on the list of smart things to do. Warmth spread through Clementine, and she moved toward the two of them, deciding to put her brother out of his misery.

"This looks great, guys."

They both turned to stare at her with wide, guilty eyes. Then Bastien's gaze landed on his son and his entire demeanor changed. He lit up from the inside, like his whole life was complete, then leaned in to give Jamie a kiss on the top of his bundled up little head.

Both Bastien and Anais had been talking about having kids for as long as she could remember. It must have something to do with being the oldest. The same desire had never manifested itself in Clementine. While she loved her nephew and would dote on Anais and Jackson's kid with as much auntie energy as she could, there was only panic when she thought of her family expecting the same from her.

Her eyes met Austin's, and like always, he seemed to know what she was thinking.

"Is there anything else you need from me, Bastien? I can walk Clementine and Jamie back to your place before Gabby gets home."

"Yeah, Ashleigh should be here soon. Thanks again for your help." He held out his hand, which Austin stared at for a beat before he shook it.

They walked away from Bastien, and Clementine wasn't entirely sure how she was still upright. The mess of emotions bouncing around in her body was enough to make her want to wail like Jamie would the second she stopped moving.

"Have you been walking around all morning?"

"He cries whenever I stop."

"You should have put him in his stroller."

"There's snow everywhere. This is more practical."

"You're going to tip over."

"Gabby doesn't."

"She has practice. She does this every day."

"Well, if you think you can do it better…"

"Of course I could. But you're the one who volunteered."

The back and forth was so familiar, so comforting, it was all Clementine could do to not burst into tears.

"Do you really think all of that?"

She didn't look at him, but she heard him inhale slowly. Of course he knew what she was talking about. He always did.

"I do."

"I don't need you to defend me against my family."

"I know you don't. But I want to."

She stared at him for a few moments, unsure of how she felt. Was she angry or thrilled? Touched or annoyed?

"Can I buy you a hot chocolate?"

He blinked, then a slow smile spread across his face. "Right now?"

"Well, once I return the baby to his mom." She looked down at Jamie, who was, amazingly, asleep. "When the festival opens."

"I'd like that." He took her hand in his, and even though there were layers of gloves between them, she felt the warmth of his skin on hers. "But you should spend the time with your family at the festival since you won't be here for Christmas."

"Um, they may not know about the trip yet."

He stopped walking and turned to her, the look of surprise on his face tinged with panic. She'd never seen that expression on his face before.

"What do you mean they don't know? I thought that's why Bastien was so ornery today about me and you."

"Ornery? What decade are you from, Dino?"

Instead of responding, his blue eyes stayed fixed on her, waiting. She sighed.

"I just don't know how to say it. It didn't feel like the right time at Thanksgiving, with Anais making her announcement. And it really puts the pressure on. Going with you for Christmas means they'll be thinking an engagement announcement is coming next."

It wasn't what she was really worried about, but she knew if she told him she was worried about missing her family, then he'd tell her she didn't have to go. And she wanted to go. She wanted to be there for Austin the way he'd been for her these past few weeks.

This was what she'd wanted after all, wasn't it? Being in a real relationship meant making compromises.

For once, Austin didn't seem to be reading her thoughts, or Clementine was sure he'd have called her out on the half truth she'd just told him. Instead, he ran a finger along her cheek, making her shiver. "We'll figure it out. But you'd better get me a giant hot chocolate."

By the time they delivered Jamie to a very relaxed-looking Gabby, the festival was open and in full swing. Austin would have preferred to head home, spending a cozy weekend inside with Clementine, but his girlfriend—it was embarrassing how much he loved that word attached to her name—wanted to buy him a hot chocolate. Since he was happiest when she was happy, logically he should ensure she could do what she wanted.

As usual, the Winter Wonderland in Jasper Creek's town square was wonderful, and Austin grudgingly knew it was all because of Bastien. He'd taken a step back for the Fall Festival, but making his baby's first Christmas magical—even if Jamie would not remember a thing—seemed to be his mission. The bit Austin had done was nothing compared to the hours Bastien had spent on it.

After getting his promised giant hot chocolate, Austin walked around, hand in hand, with a beaming Clementine, beyond pleased to have a reason to be touching her in public that wasn't to catch Mark's attention or put on a show for the nosy citizens of Jasper Creek. They were really doing this. Even if it was still practice for her in a way, even if he'd made sure she had an easy out that wouldn't make things hard for her, she wasn't thinking about anyone else but him.

At least, he assumed so.

"Did you tell your colleagues about the festival?" Austin asked as they strolled through the tinsel- and holly-covered booths around Town Square he'd help set up early that morning.

"No..." She bit her lip like she had more she wanted to say, but stayed quiet. Hope flickered in his chest.

"Have you done anything with your social media idea yet?"

Her eyes shot to his, wide and surprised, then she shook her head. "You remembered?"

"Of course." Dread wrapped around him when he realized what her question meant. "Has he not brought it up again?"

Mark's name was hanging there, unsaid but implied, in the air between them. They hadn't mentioned him once since Clementine had said that Mark might not be who she thought he was. Whatever that meant. No matter how much mental gymnastics Austin had done, he hadn't been able to work out what Clementine thought of her boss now. Of course, he could ask her, but then she'd know just how much he cared about the answer. How much he cared about her. It wouldn't be fair to put that kind of pressure on her in her first relationship.

If all he was going to be was her first, then he wanted to do things perfectly. He'd show her how a boyfriend should treat her, make sure her expectations were sky high for whatever lucky guy who was smart enough to ask her out.

Admitting he didn't want their relationship to end if she didn't want the same would just make him the selfish jerk he'd been with Cassidy. No, Clementine would get the clean break she deserved, and Austin would figure out a way to be okay.

Before she could answer the question he had actually asked, he spotted Anais and Jackson, looking deliriously happy as they strolled through the booths, sipping hot chocolate and enjoying their last festival as just the two of them. When he caught Jackson's eye, the two couples moved slowly toward each other.

There was at least one thing that could get resolved today.

"You might as well tell her now." He bent low to say the words in Clementine's ear, breathing her in.

She tensed next to him. "We didn't even talk about what to say."

"Don't worry." He put his arm around her shoulders. "You'll figure it out."

"Sometimes, it would be nice to not care what they think." She leaned into him and sighed, the simplicity and familiarity of it wrapping his chest in a vise.

"You don't care, not really."

She glanced up at him, her eyebrows furrowed.

"I mean, you clearly want them to think a certain way about you. Which is totally normal." He gave her shoulders a reassuring squeeze. "You're not a sociopath, after all. Always nice in a girlfriend."

This got a small tilt of her lips.

"You want her approval. Also normal. But you've acted without it before, and everything turned out fine."

"You mean PT school."

"I'm sure there are other examples."

She was quiet for a moment, her brow furrowed and lips turned down in a frown. "Yeah, there are a few."

"So just tell her. Whatever she thinks, it'll be fine."

There were a hundred different emotions that flashed across her face by the time her sister and Jackson finally made their way over to them.

"Hey, you two." Anais was beaming like she had been at work every day for the past few weeks.

She'd told her news to Hunter and Jane, the other two members of the staff at Miller Family Medical, the Monday after Thanksgiving, and nothing seemed to bother her since. If Clementine was going to tell her sister about the trip to California, this would be the best time.

Assuming she'd be able to get the words out. When Austin looked over at her, she was as frozen as the air around them.

"Enjoying the festival?" He rubbed his hand on Clementine's arm, reminding her he was there for her. He hoped she knew that he'd always be there.

"It's incredible. Bastien really outdid himself. I can't wait to see what he ends up doing at their house this year." Anais chuckled. "Minnie, are you okay doing presents there this year instead of Mom and Dad's? It's probably easier for us to go there than for Bastien to lug everything over."

"Um." Her eyes shot to Austin, and he just gave her a smile and a small shake of his head. He wasn't going to do this for her. She could do it.

The instant she realized the same thing, her shoulders dropped, and her chin lifted. Shaking out her hair, she took a deep breath.

If he hadn't already been halfway in love with her, he would have fallen right then and there.

"Actually, Austin invited me to California to spend Christmas with his family." It wasn't a question. She wasn't asking permission. She was telling her sister what she wanted and her tone left no room for negotiation or discussion.

"Oh." Eyebrows raised, Anais glanced at Jackson, then at Austin. Slowly, a smile spread across her lips. "That's great, Minnie. You'll have a lot fun."

"Really?" All the strength left her voice in a rush of air.

"Well, I assume you'll have fun." Now she narrowed her eyes at Austin. "He never says much about them, so you'll have to be my spy. Get all the inside info on the Gibson clan I haven't been able to."

"Um, sure. Of course." Clementine's eyes cut to Austin, who kept his face blank.

"I don't know what you're talking about, Anais. I've told you plenty. It's not my fault if you're just not a good listener."

"Oh, stop it." She flapped her hand at him like he was a misbehaving animal, and he chuckled. "Be careful with your shoulder. It's still not fully healed. Minnie, you'll take care of him, right?"

Clementine nodded, still looking somewhat shell-shocked.

"I need another hot chocolate," Anais said. "You two coming?"

Austin shook his head. "I've had my fill."

"Okay, have fun." She waved and walked off with Jackson. "See you Monday, Austin. Minnie, call me if you need help packing."

There were a few minutes of silence before Clementine turned to him, eyes wide.

"Did that just happen?"

"No, you hit your head and hallucinated the whole thing." He smirked, pride swelling in his chest.

She wrapped her arms around him, the hug warming him more than the hot chocolate had. "Thank you."

"I didn't do anything. That was all you."

It was amazing. The change she'd already been through, and now this final step. It was like watching some rare flower bloom in front of him, and he was blessed just to be there on the full moon when it happened.

Austin could only hope that he'd get the chance to see it again, as often as he could, until she finally figured out what she wanted. If it turned out it wasn't him, he might be able to survive, knowing she'd never be the timid Clementine ever again.

"You said it would be fine. I should have listened to you." Her head was against his chest and her arms around him. There was snow on the ground and a chill in the air. It was the perfect winter moment with the perfect woman.

"You should listen to yourself, Cutie. That's the whole point."

"I wish you'd been there a few years ago when I told them about getting my DPT." They pulled out of the embrace and started walking again, hand in hand, around the snowy Town Square.

"I take it things didn't go as smoothly?" He'd gotten bits and pieces of the conversation from Anais, but mostly he remembered the stress it had caused her in the weeks after, the panic that everything she'd planned for Miller Family Medical wouldn't work out. Even Austin's reassurance hadn't done much to calm her, at least not at first. Some things just took time to realize it wasn't as much of a disaster as you thought it was.

Clementine laughed, a hollow sound in the cold winter air. "Not really."

"Why did you do it?"

She bit her lip. "I don't want to be like them. Not because they're not great. I just... don't feel like we're the same."

This hadn't been the answer he'd expected. He thought she'd mention her blood phobia, which she never talked about. But Clementine insisted on amazing him at every opportunity.

He brushed some of her hair back from her face where it had escaped her hat. "I get it. You'll see why once we're in California."

"Can't you at least give me a hint?" She stuck out her lower lip and his chest caved in a little. The day she realized just how irresistible she was would likely be his final one on earth.

Smoothing out his expression, he raised an eyebrow. "Does that look ever work?"

"All the time on Bastien. Less on Anais. It's fifty-fifty with my parents."

That's what he would have expected.

"A hint?" He took her hand in his and they kept walking. "I have two sisters and a brother. All younger than me."

"The oldest?" Clementine waved at someone as they passed a wreath-making booth. "I believe I already guessed that."

He nudged her shoulder with his. They were almost to the edge of the festival and would have to turn around if they wanted to stay longer. "Alright, smarty-pants. Now what else do you want to see today?"

She listed off her favorite things to do at the festival, and they spent the day together exploring them all. When Clementine knew what she wanted, she was irresistible.

Now if only what she really wanted was him, things would be perfect.

TWENTY-ONE
CLEMENTINE

As Clementine dragged her suitcase into the staff break room, there was only one thing on her mind.

Austin.

They'd spent the rest of the Winter Festival walking around, hand in hand. The kiss he'd given her when he dropped her off had been lingering, his hand smoothing its way through her hair and coming to rest on the nape of her neck like he never wanted to let go.

The idea that he might not want it to end either was enticing, but she didn't want to say anything until she was sure. Was this really what she wanted? Was it what he wanted? Was she an idiot for thinking this could be something really real?

A week with Austin's family would certainly answer some of those questions.

"Whoa, it looks like you're never coming back." Mark appeared in the break room, a look of concern on his face as he leaned against the doorway.

"Oh no, it's just big because of the ski pants and everything." She shoved it into a corner as best she could. Anais had been more than generous with her opinions on what she should pack, and while Clementine didn't think she'd need eight cocktail dresses, it had been easier to put them in her suitcase than argue. Some things would never change between Clementine and her sister, no matter how many fearless declarations she managed with Austin's help. "I'm sorry for bringing it here, but I won't have time to go home after work, and there's some beer from the Floodline in it that I don't want to freeze while it sits in the car all day. I hope this is okay?"

A panicked jolt hit her stomach. If this had been some plan to get Mark's attention, then she would be thrilled right now. But she wasn't thinking about Mark. She was worried about Austin's family not liking her. Which was ridiculous, since they weren't actually together.

But technically they were. Or could be. Or something.

"It's fine. You're not spending the holidays with your family?"

She shook her head. "Heading to California with Austin right after work to spend it with his."

Mark's eyebrows shot up. "That seems really fast."

A few weeks ago, the concern or jealousy or whatever it was on his face would have thrilled Clementine. Instead, she had that familiar streak of irritation snaking its way through her chest and winding itself around her lungs to steal her breath. Someone giving their opinion on her dating life where she hadn't asked for it. Her siblings finally seemed on board, so what was Mark's issue? At the bar, he'd been worried about her leaving if Austin broke her heart. But he was her boss, not a friend giving dating advice.

"Even if we've only been dating a few months, I've known him much longer." She turned to face him and put her hands on her hips.

"That's the best way to start things, isn't it? Friends first." He had a sweet look on his face, and despite her excitement over her upcoming trip with Austin, her heart beat faster to see him looking at her that way.

"It is."

He smiled, eyes bright, and headed for the door. "Well, I hope everything goes well for you. I'm here if things don't and you need to talk about it, okay?"

That was a weird thing to say. "Um, thanks."

There was something else there, under the surface, but her frazzled nerves couldn't figure out where to even begin. Did he really hope the trip would go well, or was he hoping it wouldn't? What did that comment about being friends first mean?

She decided to bring things back around to something professional, something she was sure she wanted. That's what had made the difference with Anais, with everything. Once she knew what she wanted, nothing could get in her way. "Maybe when I get back, we can talk about some other ideas I have for the clinic, since you don't think the social media one will work?"

"Oh, sure." He checked his watch. "Sounds like a plan. If I don't see you before you go, have a good trip."

"You too." The second he was out the door, she smacked her hand on her forehead.

You too? She hadn't even asked him what he was doing over the holidays. Since her dad closed down Miller Family Medical for the week between Christmas and New Year's, it was usually her favorite time of year, full of family time and long, lingering breakfasts. Everyone else in her family had reacted the same way as Anais at the news Clementine would be spending the holiday in California. The pressure of disappointing them was gone. This year there would be little Jamie there with them, and while she was disappointed to miss his first Christmas, there was more at stake here than a cute photo op that only the adults would remember.

By the time they got back from the trip, they'd either be something more, something real, or their fake-turned-sort-of-real relationship would have ended.

She had no idea which outcome she wanted more.

Clementine knew she'd gotten more determined over the past few years, and especially the past few months. Or rather, she'd always been that way and recently was finding the courage to act on it.

It was hard to go for something, however, if you didn't know what it was.

As she went about her day, the work a welcome distraction from her nerves about the upcoming trip, an idea started to form. It was a devious one, and Austin was probably too smart to fall for it, but it would settle things one way or another.

She needed to see if she could make Austin jealous. Of Mark.

While her next patient went through their last series of dead-lifts to strengthen their hamstrings after knee surgery, Clementine worked out the details. They'd gone weeks without discussing her boss, not since she'd admitted to Austin that Mark might not be the guy she thought he was and then asked Austin if they could date for real.

Was making your boyfriend jealous to see if he liked you as much as you liked him something a real girlfriend would do? She had no idea. She wasn't about to ask either of her sisters. One thing she did know was that she couldn't just ask Austin outright what he wanted. He was so attuned to her needs, to supporting her, that he would take it as a sign that she wasn't interested. If she admitted how strong her feelings had gotten, and he didn't feel the same, he'd probably leave Jasper Creek just to make sure things didn't get awkward for her.

It was better to know for sure how he felt before she said anything.

Apparently, Clementine got airsick. Austin spent the first half of the flight with his hand on her back, feeling like the biggest jerk in the world. Of all the ways she could surprise him, this wasn't something he'd ever wanted.

"I didn't even think about this." He pushed the button for the flight attendant, who appeared in an instant. The calm smile on his face did little to settle Austin's racing pulse. "I didn't bring anything for her. Do you have something that might help?"

The flight attendant nodded, then disappeared for a moment, back with some ginger chew candies that Clementine took one look at and turned even paler.

"You can't predict everything." Clementine moaned, her forehead shining with sweat and the airsickness bag clutched in her hand.

"I should have at least been prepared." He held out the candies, and she opened her mouth to let him pop one in. "Chew please."

Some of the worry left him when she rolled her eyes at him. If she was able to do that, then she'd survive. "Just distract me."

He could do that.

"Have you really not been to California?"

"Just for Bastien's graduation. We don't travel much. Five kids, you know?" She settled back in her seat. The first-class section of the small plane from Denver to Bishop wasn't what he usually booked, but when he found out Clementine had only been in a plane once, he'd wanted to make sure this trip went well.

So far, he was failing at that. Failing wasn't something he was used to, and he did his best to ignore the slow, premonitory creep of dread that was clawing at his chest.

"Didn't your mom want to take you all to France?" All of the Miller children had French names, thanks to Dr. Heather Miller's love for the country and culture. He'd heard the story once from Anais that her dad planned to take her for their honeymoon, but then she'd gotten pregnant with the twins and that had been put on hold.

"She wanted to, and she'll get there eventually, but I don't know that we all have to go."

"I took you to be an explorer."

The plane shook with some turbulence and her cheeks puffed out. "Not if it's like this."

"It's a smaller plane. Bigger ones are smoother."

"Would it be a bigger one to go to New York?"

"Yes."

"That's the only place I've ever really wanted to visit."

That wasn't what he thought she'd say. There was a faint line of sweat around her hairline, so he wanted to keep her talking, keep her distracted. "Why?"

"It has everything. Theater, museums, parks, beaches."

"Long Island is not a beach."

Closing her eyes, she leaned back in her seat, looking slightly less pale. "What a Californian thing to say. I take it you grew up near the beach?"

"Yes." It had been easy enough to avoid her questions before, but now that they were actually going, she had to know at least some basics about him. It had felt like he might jinx it if he told her too much beforehand. "Pacific Palisades."

There was no flicker of recognition, and Austin felt even more of his worry melt away.

He had good reason to be on edge, given everything that had happened with Cassidy. And before her, his med school girlfriend. If Clementine didn't realize just what it meant to grow up where he had, then he wasn't going to be the one to tell her. She'd find out soon enough.

"You go to Mammoth Mountain every winter?"

"Since I was five."

"It's nice to have those kinds of traditions." Breathing deeply, her eyes shifted down for a moment and his chest clenched. Asking her to spend the holidays away from her family for the first time couldn't be that easy. He hadn't believed for a second that she'd held off on telling them about the trip because of the pressure it would put on him. Clearly she wished she could be with them, but she'd chosen to come with him.

Now she was sick.

He put his hand on top of hers. "Thank you for coming with me. I know you're missing a lot."

Her eyes were on his hand, not his face, when she responded. "I'm happy to try something new. Even if everyone has opinions on it."

"Oh? Did Bastien say something?"

"Um, no. Mark did."

There was a sharp stab in the middle of Austin's chest that confounded him. After all, Clementine was the one who had chosen to stop pursuing Mark. She wanted to date Austin, even if on a deadline. So why did her sudden mention of her boss make Austin want to bang his head against the plane's window?

"Right. Well, what did you expect? He still hates me."

She nodded and slipped her hand out of his. The stabbing pain in his chest increased tenfold.

Just like Cassidy, she was coming on this trip with ulterior motives, and he had to remember that. They might not be the same unscrupulous reasons as his ex, but they were just as likely to break his heart.

She turned to the window and didn't say much the rest of the flight. Once they had landed and retrieved their bags, Clementine kept the window open in the car all the way to the rental house. It was freezing, but Austin didn't complain. At least her skin had lost its pale, greenish tint.

As he drove the car through the winding snow-covered mountain paths in the deep winter evening light, Austin felt the familiar sense of calm wash over him.

"Are all the houses here this big?"

"Hmm?" He looked over at her to find her nibbling her lips, eyes wide and taking in the endless sea of lights in the chalets dotting the side of the mountain. "These are all rentals. For families."

This didn't seem to satisfy her, but she didn't ask any more questions. The calm he'd felt earlier was slowly dripping away like melting icicles.

They pulled into the largest house at the top of the road, and he turned off the engine. He shifted in his seat, then cleared his throat. If he didn't do it now, she'd be completely unprepared for what she was about to see. "So I didn't want to bother you with this on the plane..."

Her head whipped around to his, and her skin paled. She briefly closed her eyes and breathed in deeply before opening them again. "Does it have something to do with the mansion we just pulled up in front of?"

"It's not a mansion."

"It has a guest house." She pointed to a smaller chalet on one side of the main house.

Austin pursed his lips, struggling to find the words he knew he should have said weeks ago. She sat back in her seat and kept her eyes on him, waiting.

Like ripping off a bandage, he let the words tumble out of him. "My whole family is in show business."

A few blinks of her beautiful dark eyes and her shoulders dropped. "Oh. Okay."

Had she been expecting something horrible? The smallest flicker of hope made its way through his chest.

"My brother's an actor." He took a deep breath, bracing himself. Back in his teens and early twenties, he'd never been this nervous around bringing girlfriends home. But that was before his little brother Hayden had gone from adorable child actor into superstar celebrity and everything had changed for his family. "Hayden Carmichael."

Her eyes went wide. "That kid from *Escape to New York?*"

"He has done a few things since then." His lips turned up, pleased that she wasn't the superfan like so many women her age were. He knew Anais loved movies, even had a whole ice cream pairing system set up, so he'd never mentioned it to her. When someone asked what his family did, it was easy enough to glide over the relevant information and present something more neutral.

"You said your parents were lawyers."

He'd admitted to this much when she was picking out a gift for them earlier in the week.

"They are. For a movie studio."

"And your siblings do 'this and that' but don't really need to work."

"Also true. We all have trust funds."

Clementine glared at him. "This isn't funny. I'm completely unprepared."

"You know their names." He smoothed a hand over the steering wheel and avoided looking at her.

"You said your brother's name is Charlie." She didn't sound mad exactly, more... confused. Hurt, even. How to explain that he kept all of this to himself for reasons that had nothing to do with her and everything to do with his own complicated feelings about his family?

"It is. His agent is the one who suggested using his middle name and my mother's maiden name as his stage name. To keep the rest of the family out of the spotlight."

Really to keep Austin out of it. The rest of them worked in show business too, but by the time his little brother had landed his first major role, Austin was already pre-med and wanted to keep his life as separate as possible from theirs.

He knew from the shift in Clementine's expression that he would pay for this later. It was beyond satisfying to see her devious nature kick in instead of fear or anxiety. Better for her to be angry at him for hiding the truth than quivering with nerves in front of his little brother. Who might not even be there, given how unpredictable he was. The last time he'd gotten a text from him, he'd been in love with some model he'd met on a photo shoot and followed her to Spain for a few months.

After a moment of silence in the car when all he could hear was the pounding of his heart in his ears, her eyebrows arched playfully. "So are you the big disappointment in the family?"

"Disappointment? Me?" He gratefully slipped back into their comfortable, teasing roles.

"Just a doctor, not a movie star or... What do your sisters do?"

"Olivia is a stylist for movies, does some designing as well, and Ava is a junior agent."

"How did none of us know about this?" She shook her head, sounding bemused. "You've known Anais for years. The fact that your family is a big deal in Hollywood never came up?"

He shrugged, knowing she should hear the whole story but there wasn't enough time right now. Not when they were all waiting just on the other side of the front door. "Your family's more interesting."

The look she gave him could have melted the snow off the

mountain. He laughed and leaned back in his seat. "It's been a source of... tension with previous girlfriends. So I learned to keep it quiet until I can really trust someone."

"You trust me more than Anais? Or Gabby?" Her hand made its way to squeeze his on top of the console between them. The warmth of it was reassuring, and he allowed himself to share a little more than he'd been planning to.

"What my family does isn't relevant to my day-to-day life. They hear stories all the time about my sisters and from when my brother was little. But some parts of my life I like to keep separate."

"I get that."

"I know you do, Cutie. That's why you're here."

Her lip turned up, teasing again, but her words were the last thing he'd expected. "I thought I was here because this is what you got in return for helping me with Mark."

The name was like a punch to the chest. It was the second time she'd mentioned him today after weeks of nothing. Even if she didn't seem to be interested in Mark anymore, the name set off some irrational internal reaction in him. It reminded him that his time with Clementine was limited. Austin might be her boyfriend now, but this would end, and she'd move on to someone else. Even if everything he was feeling for her was growing deeper by the day.

Before he could think too hard about it, he reached for her and planted a kiss on her mouth. Some far corner of his reptilian brain wanted to erase the mention of any other man from her lips. As the kiss grew deeper, she clung to him, and their breaths and lips mingled until it was hard to know where he stopped and she began. She had to feel something more, or she wouldn't be here at all. Right?

But he'd grown up in Hollywood, and he'd been fooled by fakes before.

TWENTY-THREE
CLEMENTINE

Standing in front of the biggest front door she'd ever seen, Clementine had approximately thirty seconds to get used to the idea that she was about to meet Hayden Carmichael. If it had been Austin's intention to distract her from her nerves around meeting his glamorous family with the kiss to end all kisses, then he'd mostly succeeded.

She was also around sixty percent sure that bringing up Mark had stirred some jealousy. But sixty wasn't one hundred, and she wasn't about to put her heart at risk for those odds quite yet.

Luckily, instead of his famous brother, it was one of Austin's sisters who opened the door. Blond and sparkling, she looked exactly what you'd expect from a movie star's sister, and the opposite of how she'd pictured Austin's family until a few minutes ago.

"It's so nice to meet you! I'm Olivia. I've heard so much about you." His sister leaned forward to give her shoulders a squeeze and plant air kisses near her cheeks. Austin had already walked in, and from over Olivia's shoulder, he rolled his eyes and shook his head. Some of the tension in Clementine's stomach relaxed.

"Only the bad things I hope." Clementine smirked and winked

at Austin, whose shoulders dropped like he'd been worried too. "This is a beautiful house. Thank you for inviting me."

"Like we'd say no when Austin finally brings someone after so many years." A second sparkly blonde appeared, almost identical to Olivia but with a short bob instead of long waves.

Austin bent to give his sister a hug. "Maybe I just didn't want to subject them to your interrogations."

"It's not my fault if we need to be careful." Olivia gave her a smile that was just a shade too cool to be friendly. "Lots of gold diggers and fakes in show business. I'm sure you understand."

Fakes. Her heart skipped a beat. "Well, if it helps, I had no idea who any of you were until about three minutes ago."

"Austin! You didn't even tell her about my new line of bags for Kate Spade?" Spinning on her high heels, Olivia shot a glare at him, then turned back to Clementine, all smiles. "Just let me know your favorite color and I'll get you whatever you want."

"Blue," she replied without even thinking. Her gaze slid to Austin, who was shaking his head at his sisters.

"Oh, just like his eyes, right?" Ava gave her a nudge. "He did get the good eyes. Could have been an actor, but he wanted to put that giant brain to use."

If Clementine hadn't grown up with siblings, it would have been overwhelming. She could see why Austin had been nervous to bring her, and she could easily imagine that it hadn't always gone very well in the past.

"Brain? Honestly, all I've noticed so far are the eyes."

His sisters cackled while Austin sighed in that exasperated way that only a guy with multiple sisters ever did. Clementine had heard it more times than she could count from Bastien and Eli.

"Oh, I think she'll do just fine." Ava winked at her, and the only thing keeping it from feeling like a victory was the fact that Clementine's relationship with Austin had technically started as fake. Just not the kind they seemed to be worried about.

"Are they here? Someone could have told us." A tall, imposingly handsome woman with her silver hair in a pixie cut appeared at the end of the long entry hall.

Austin wrapped her in a hug, then turned with a proud expression on his face.

"Clementine, this is my mom, Nicole Gibson. Mom, this is Clementine Miller."

Nicole's silver eyebrows drew together, and she extended a hand for Clementine to shake. "Austin tells us you're another doctor?"

"Physical therapist." Somewhere in the back of Clementine's brain, she'd known that Austin's ex was a doctor who worked at CUH, but she'd managed to forget it until now. Until she was suddenly "another" one of Austin's girlfriends he'd brought home for the holidays and would be compared to them. She lifted her chin and straightened her back, faking the confidence she was suddenly so desperately lacking.

"Oh well, that's much more interesting." His mother's eyes lit up.

"Is it?" That wasn't what most people said.

"Ours just retired."

Austin was shaking his head and wagging his finger. "She isn't here to work, Mom."

"No, no, of course not..." But there was a shrewd look in her eyes, one that Clementine had seen in Austin's more than once. There was some major contriving happening in her head, and Clementine would have laughed if she didn't think that would somehow lose her points.

Then, like she'd imagined the whole thing, Austin's mom put on a warm smile that was the mirror image of the one on her daughters' faces. "You must be exhausted. You two are in the bedroom upstairs all the way at the end of the hall. Dinner should be ready in an hour, but we'll have drinks beforehand if you want to come down early." His mom drifted off in the direction of the kitchen, followed closely by Ava and Olivia, chatting away.

It took her a moment to process everything that had just happened, and that Hayden had yet to make an appearance. She wasn't entirely sure if that made it easier or not.

"They seem… nice?"

"You'll get used to it." With a chuckle, Austin picked up their bags and headed toward the wide, sweeping staircase lined with holly and twinkling lights. "Let's go, Cutie."

"Wait." Her heart stopped. It actually stopped beating in her chest, her entire body seizing up. "We're sharing a room?"

He turned and the smirk on his face disappeared when he saw she was frozen at the bottom of the stairs. "Relax. We're not doing anything other than sleeping."

"Oh. Right, of course."

"Unless you… wanted to?" He raised an eyebrow, more surprised than suggestive.

The heat was so intense in her face she thought she was melting. "No, thank you."

He chuckled and shook his head, then continued his journey up the stairs. "Don't worry, Cutie, I'm sure there's a couch. It'll all be quite proper."

Her feet stumbled on the first step. Would a real boyfriend want to keep things proper? The heat in her face made its way down her arms, and her palms began to sweat. She was way out of her depth with Austin. Not just this one bed conundrum—that she honestly should have predicted—but also with his family. They were nice, nicer than she'd expected, based on how tight-lipped he'd been about them. Now everything she'd seen hinted at a world so very different from the small one she lived in.

Even if he did feel something more for her, something even half as what she was feeling for him, she suddenly wasn't sure she could be what he would be expecting long-term.

"Clementine?" Austin appeared at the top of the stairs, his beautiful features pulled into a concerned frown. When she didn't answer, just stared at him helplessly on the bottom step, he rushed down and slipped his arms around her. "Are you still sick from the flight?"

She shook her head and leaned into him, breathing in his smell, still crisp and cold from the open window in the car. "It's just a lot."

He planted a single, sweet kiss on her forehead. "I know they're a lot." It wasn't what she'd meant, but she was enjoying the warmth of his arms and the kiss too much to say anything. "You really will get used to them. I promise. And if you don't, we can go home early and spend Christmas with your family like I know you really want to."

If she hadn't already been halfway in love with him, then this would have done it. She might not know much about dating or kissing or impressing a boyfriend's family, but she knew with one hundred percent certainty that this wonderful man was going to completely shatter her.

———

As usual, Austin was right. About everything.

She got used to his family, their shallow yet somehow genuine way of talking, their fixation on discussing the people they knew and what was happening in Hollywood. It was their job, after all, and it was different from working in medicine, where you had to keep everything private. It was fascinating, really, to hear so much about the inner workings of how movies got made and how reputations could rise and fall with a single piece of gossip.

Maybe it was because Mr. and Mrs. Gibson were lawyers, but none of it seemed to cross any lines into industry secrets about current projects. Anytime something about what Hayden was working on next or a title of a film Clementine hadn't even realized was being made came up, one of Austin's parents would give a tight little nod of their head and the conversation would switch quickly to something else. They were so good at this, she stopped noticing after a while. There was plenty to hear about past movies and fading stars to keep their conversations entertaining.

Austin had also been right about there being a couch in the bedroom. It was where he slept, though he always went to bed after her and woke up before she did, giving her as much time and space alone in the room as she wanted.

Nothing he'd said had prepared her for the skiing, however.

She'd been worried that Austin would try to push himself when his shoulder wasn't fully healed, but skiing with the Gibsons wasn't quite the same as it was everywhere else. For starters, they spent more time in the lodge than actually skiing, and his sisters invited her to the village to visit shops and restaurants. If they didn't go out in the evenings, they had people over to their house. The cocktail dresses Anais had insisted she needed to pack came in handy after all—not that she'd admit that to her sister anytime soon.

It felt like everyone there was someone famous, and his parents seemed to know all of them. Or one of his sisters worked with them, or Hayden had done a movie with them.

The way they introduced Austin with so much pride was adorable, and Clementine found herself wrapped up in that. The second anyone found out Clementine was a PT, she got asked about everything from neck pain to using physical therapy as prevention rather than rehabilitation.

Between the way they reacted to her and how everyone's eyes lit up at the word *doctor* like they'd just found their own personal dispensary, it was incredible they made it through their days on the mountain without getting job offers.

Though Clementine had a feeling if any offers did happen, they would all go through his parents. They were very invested in their children's careers, making sure to mention at least one, if not all, of their children in every conversation. Even Austin. Though they had less direct involvement in what he did, they'd drop little bits of advice to him, updating him of the value of some piece of real estate he apparently owned, or letting him know that a doctor they knew would be in Denver for a lecture on something he was interested in.

Hayden didn't show up until the day before Christmas, and he was just as charming as he seemed in movies, just a bit more inattentive than the rest of the family. Though she tried her best not to stare at him, she did notice that while the rest of the family would be talking, he'd be gazing off into the distance, his fingers tapping away at the arm of his chair, a dreamy expression on his face.

When she asked Austin about it, he just shook his head slightly and said, "youngest child" with a smile on his face, like that explained everything.

And in a way, it did. It wasn't hard to see that Hayden had been both the most spoiled and had the most pressure put on him. He reminded her of her own little brother Eli in some ways.

It also wasn't hard to see why Austin had wanted to live somewhere other than California. There was love between the Gibsons, just a different kind than Clementine had grown up with. His dad wasn't warm and generous like Dr. James Miller III, but he was brilliant and expected great things from his kids. There was an undercurrent of competition among the siblings that was just a little too intense for her to fully relax.

Still, it was hard not to enjoy herself. They were all so charming and smart, it was easy for Clementine to start to love them, too, which she knew she shouldn't. After all, this wasn't real. When the vacation was over, when the New Year rolled around, her relationship with Austin would end. Unless she found a way to tell him that she was falling for him and didn't want to break up...

But that was something for future Clementine to deal with. Today was Christmas Eve, and she was putting on her makeup before dinner with just the family, while Austin was doing something fiddly with his tie.

She could see him behind her in the mirror and caught his eye. "Your family is lovely."

"You sound surprised." A slow smile crept across his face, one she now knew was the same as Hayden and their dad.

"I thought they'd all be..."

"Pompous assholes like me?"

She rolled her eyes and leaned forward to check her mascara. "You're not an asshole."

He laughed, a bright bark of a sound that warmed her chest. "But I am pompous?"

"Well, it's not like you don't have a reason to be."

"Is that a compliment? Be still my heart."

She turned to face him, suddenly wanting to be serious. "I'm sorry if I don't say it much, but you are incredible, Austin. I hope you don't think meeting your family changes how impressive I find you."

He opened his smirking mouth to say something, then seemed to notice her expression and closed it, swallowing hard. "Thank you."

"You've just been so... generous with me." The whole trip he'd taken every opportunity to talk her up, and when he'd mentioned her social media idea to Olivia, Clementine had gotten a crash course in online marketing that had lasted for over two hours and included a tutorial on filming videos. Even if Mark would never want her to use it, it had sparked all sorts of new ideas for Clementine about what might be possible for her career as a PT.

"Well, you are my girlfriend."

"Not for much longer."

He sucked in a breath, and her heart beat wildly in her ears. There was a depth in his gaze she'd never seen before, fanning the flames of the silent hope she'd clung to in those moments where she felt the most powerful, the most attractive, like all his looks and touches might actually be signs of something deeper.

But he didn't say anything.

She turned back to the mirror to put in her earrings. "Anyway, whatever the reason, I want to return the favor."

"You don't have to." He stepped into the bathroom—larger than Clementine's entire bedroom at home—and leaned against the second sink.

"Because your ego is big enough as it is?" Her lips twitched.

"No, because I don't deserve someone like you."

Her hand stopped halfway through putting on the second earring. It was hard to ignore his expression in the bright lights of the vanity. She took a deep breath before turning to him, finally asking what she'd been wondering about for weeks.

"What happened with Cassidy? You said she cheated, and it had to do with your family. It wasn't with someone I met?" Her heart ached just thinking about it. If she'd been friendly to someone who'd hurt him, she'd never forgive herself. "It wasn't Hayden, was it?"

He shook his head. "No, he would never do that to me."

She waited, her pulse pounding so hard she could taste it.

"Some of the people you've met skiing though..." He sighed and rubbed a hand over his face. The harsh bathroom lighting that made her hyperaware of every flaw on her face somehow only made his best features stand out more. His eyes were bluer than ever, the lines of his face sharp and sumptuous. "It's easy to get caught up in the glamor of this world if you didn't grow up in it. That's the simplest way to explain what happened with Cassidy. And my girlfriend before her."

There was a part of her that wanted the whole story, to know every detail of what had happened, but really, he'd told her enough to put together the pieces. Cassidy met his family, their friends, and decided she wanted more than the life she had with Austin in Denver.

What she didn't know was why Austin wanted that simpler, less glamorous life in Colorado.

Why he'd want someone like her.

Asking him was out of the question. He'd tell her the truth, whatever it was, and nothing about the past few days had made her one hundred percent sure he was feeling the same things as her. She'd brought up Mark every time he mentioned to someone she was a PT, and Austin's reactions had varied. Sometimes he gripped her harder, almost possessively; sometimes he didn't seem to notice at all.

"The rest of your family seems pretty caught up in the glamor though."

He leaned against the counter, his tall frame impeccable in a dark suit. "It's their jobs. It's their life, you know? With Hayden starting acting so young, he's even more disconnected from reality. His heart is there, but he just doesn't even know what it's like to live without all of this."

"But you wanted to?"

His eyes, so bright and so blue, settled on hers, and her heartbeat kicked up in a Pavlovian response she wondered if she'd ever be free of.

"I think you, of all people, can understand loving your family but wanting a life separate from them."

She did. So much. It was like wanting to split herself in half. The part of her that loved them never wanted to leave them. The part of her that loved her quiet life that had nothing to do with them was constantly at war with the first part.

"Of course I do. It's why I wanted to be a PT."

"Yes, you've said that before. Though I always thought it's because you hate blood."

"How did you know that?" Her voice was shaking, and she gripped the edge of the sink to keep herself upright.

"I pay attention, Cutie."

His eyes were boring into her like he could read every desire of her soul, and in that moment, in the harsh, unforgiving light of a giant bathroom in the middle of the Sierra Nevadas, she realized she wanted Austin. Really wanted him. More than she'd ever wanted Mark, more than she'd ever wanted anything.

A new war was now raging inside her.

Being with Austin for real would mean she'd never have her own life. She'd be wrapped up in Miller Family Medical, in life in Jasper Creek. It's what she wanted but also the last thing she wanted. With Anais and Jackson expecting, Austin would be taking on more at the clinic, and Clementine would have yet another adorable reason to stay close to her family. As much as she'd pictured her life there, it was all too easy to imagine something else for herself. This trip was showing her that you could love your family but have a life completely separate from them.

Austin wasn't the way to do that. Neither was Mark, though she thought at first he might have been, with his second practice in Denver and wanting to expand into even more cities. If Clementine was going to have the life she wanted, away from the loving but complicated dynamics she'd grown up with, it would be something she'd have to do on her own.

With a deep inhale that echoed in the cavernous bathroom, Austin took a step toward her, his gaze intent on her lips. All it took was a few subtle shifts of her body, and they were kissing. His hand was on her neck, holding her tight against him, and her lips parted, breathing him in like he was oxygen. The edge of the sink dug into her back, and when she twisted to adjust positions, he seemed to know instinctively what the problem was. He wrapped a hand around her waist and twirled them so he was against the sink.

There was a little voice in the back of her head, urging her to keep going, but a much louder one telling her this had to end or she'd always be stuck in Jasper Creek. She never wanted to stop kissing Austin, but she wanted something else more. With a shuddering breath, she pulled away and kept her eyes on the shiny tiled floor beneath her feet.

Even if Austin did want her just as much—and that was a big if since her plan to make him jealous by mentioning Mark had failed so spectacularly—a life with him in Jasper Creek wasn't the life she wanted for herself.

"Should we go downstairs?" She turned and walked out of the

bathroom without looking back to see if he was following. Without looking back to see what must be his confused, well-kissed face.

But what could she say that wouldn't somehow hurt him? They were set to break up anyway in a few days, so there was no need to say anything else now to make that harder than it had to be.

They were in the middle of a world full of fakes and liars for another few days, so that's what she'd keep doing. Pretending she felt one thing to get what she really wanted.

Austin had never been to Christmas Eve with the Millers, but he knew it had to be as different as you could get from celebrating with the Gibsons.

The food was, as always, amazing, and the decorations were picture perfect. The posts from his sisters on social media of the tree and dinner table had already gotten thousands of likes, and the single selfie Hayden shared of him with their parents would be featured on celebrity websites before they'd even finished their first course.

Halfway through dinner, Austin leaned over to whisper in Clementine's ear. "Spending Christmas away from your family isn't too hard?"

She'd been quiet all night, but at his question, she smiled, and he saw no trace of the sadness in her eyes he thought he'd seen earlier in the bathroom. Where she'd pulled out of their kiss like it was the last thing she wanted.

"I thought it would be, but it's not that different. Just a little fancier."

"And with a celebrity."

Her eyes sparked and her lips twisted into a smirk. "Well, I wasn't going to mention that part since you seem so sensitive about it..."

"I'm not." Except he was. Of course she'd have noticed his tight grip on his fork and the slight tic of a muscle in his jaw whenever his younger brother said something to Clementine and made her laugh.

Even if things were going so much better with Clementine, even if she seemed unimpressed by the celebrities she'd met over the past few days, it was hard not to worry the same thing would still happen somehow.

But did he really have reason to be concerned? After all, this was set to end next week, and until he told her he wanted it to go on longer, nothing she said or did should be considered anything other than her holding up her end of the bargain they'd made weeks ago, before he'd gone and fallen for the one person he'd never expected.

That's what he told himself, but the brush-off in the bathroom was hard to interpret any other way.

Now he wished he'd gotten her a better present to open in front of his family.

"Is it present time yet?" Ava asked as if she'd read Austin's mind.

"We usually wait until after dinner," he said, but the second he did, he knew it was a rookie mistake.

"Oh, is there something you're nervous about?" Her eyes flashed sharply between him and Clementine, a knowing smile spreading her expensively filled lips.

"Yes, I forgot to get you anything," he shot back, and she stuck her tongue out at him. "Princess."

"Brat."

"Stop it, both of you," said their father from the end of the long table.

Clementine snickered next to him. "See, not that different from the Millers," she whispered.

His lips twitched, and he led her to the living room, where there was a pile of wrapped packages underneath the professionally styled eight-foot tree.

After the gifts were passed out, everyone tore into their pile, shouting out thanks as they opened things.

Clementine bit her lip and turned to whisper to Austin. "I hope everyone likes the beer I brought them."

"A microbrewery that nobody else here will have heard of that they can only get from a single source? They'll love it." He rubbed her back, unable to stop himself from touching her, just this small amount, relieved he had the excuse that it was what was expected of them. "Here, open one of yours."

There was a small pile at her feet, and when the first box revealed a blue bag with an "OG" logo Austin recognized immediately, Clementine gasped. "Olivia, thank you. I didn't think you were serious about getting me one."

"Of course I was." She shot a dazzling smile at Clementine. "Make sure you tag me in your posts on social media when you wear it, okay?"

The corners of Clementine's lips turned up even as she pursed them to keep from laughing, and she nodded.

Ava clapped her hands together. "Open the one from Austin now."

He shot a glare at his sister, but he handed over the box, stomach twisting. The giant stuffed cat was identical to the one he'd gotten Jamie. He knew she'd know that, a callback to their invented meet cute, but this one was in the same pattern as her cat, Marbles, who was being looked after by her neighbor while she was away.

When he'd picked it out, it seemed like a cute idea, but seeing the stuffed animal actually in her hands made him feel like an idiot. Which he almost never did.

But he could be pretty stupid when he was in love.

Wait, what? His breath caught.

"That is adorable!" Olivia cried out while Clementine brushed her hand against it, petting its fake fur. "Cats are very popular this season. Did you get me one too?"

"No, I got you a weekend at that spa you like."

She gasped and rummaged through the huge pile still at her feet to unearth an envelope, then squealed again and rushed over to give him a hug. He got his sisters and mother the same thing every year, and they always loved it—and always acted surprised. It was the kind of predictably fake-yet-genuine reaction he found enormous amounts of pleasure in. This year, however, the only reaction he cared about was Clementine's.

And he had no idea what she was thinking.

"This is very sweet, thank you." Though her words were warm enough, her face was blank, and the knot in his stomach twisted even tighter. "Open yours."

Heart pounding, he reached for the brightly decorated box and tore at the paper. He opened it up and pulled out...

A giant stuffed dinosaur.

His laugh echoed off the high ceilings in the living room, and his family turned with interest to see what was so funny.

"Do you like it, Dino?" Clementine was smiling now, and there was the playful glimmer in her eye he loved so much.

He loved her.

The realization shouldn't have been such a surprise, but when had anything with Clementine been predictable?

"I love it." He caught her eye and tried to put as much meaning as he could into the words. There was a blush in her neck that was starting to make its way up to her cheeks.

"Aw, is that an Austin-saurus?" Olivia looked over from the settee she was sitting on, covered in tissue paper and empty boxes.

"A what now?" Delight streaked across Clementine's face, all hints of being flustered by Austin's words gone in a flash.

"It used to be our nickname for him when we were little." Ava scrunched up her perfect nose made even more perfect a few weeks after her sixteenth birthday. "But did you call him Dino? Is it because he's old? I told him to stop telling people he's over thirty."

The laugh from Clementine was a familiar one, and Austin couldn't help but join in.

This was so different from how they'd treated his other girl-friends. With Cassidy in particular, they'd been cooler from the beginning. It was like they could tell before even he could that she was only there for one reason, and it wasn't him.

This would just make it harder when things ended. Though they'd understand better than anyone that this had just been a deal set up to benefit both of them. It happened all the time in Holly-wood—his parents had drafted contracts for it, and his sister had arranged it for some of her clients.

But they liked Clementine. Really liked her.

And Austin loved her. Idiot that he was.

Clementine

With all the practice she'd had over the past few months, it should have been easy to pretend for the rest of the night that everything was fine. But Austin was too smart for that.

While his sisters and mother were all looking at their calendars to plan their spa day, Austin sat down next to her and put a hand around her shoulders.

"Do you really like it?"

His voice was low, and his breath tickled her ear. She shivered, and he squeezed her close to him, probably assuming she was cold.

"I do. I was worried that what I got you was too silly, but now I think I should have gotten you an even bigger one."

She felt the rumble in his chest when he chuckled, then there was a slight tightening of his muscles. Scooting out of his arm, she turned to look at him. "Is your shoulder okay?"

"Yeah, I think I just went too hard on the weights yesterday." He hadn't been skiing, as per her recommendation, but he had been doing the exercises her colleague had given him.

"Let me take a look."

"It's fine, Cutie." He glared at her. She ignored him.

"I can tell it's not fine."

"Because you have X-ray vision now?"

"I don't. Take off your shirt."

"Oh, do we need to leave the two of you alone?" The sound of Olivia's voice was like a bucket of cold water on Clementine's head. Looking around, she realized all eyes were on her and Austin, everyone wearing identical bemused expressions at their exchange. She started to tremble and gripped the stuffed cat she still had in her hands to hide it as best she could.

In an instant, Austin was at her side. "I thought you all had a party to go to tonight at the Henderson's?"

His mom looked at her watch and nodded. "He's right. Are you sure you can't join us, Austin?"

They'd agreed the day before, when Clementine had admitted to Austin that her introverted self needed some time to recuperate, that they'd stay behind after dinner and presents while his family went to a Christmas Eve party with their longtime friends. At the time, she'd been grateful for a night off from the endlessly entertaining but equally exhausting Hollywood gossip.

Now she regretted it, not knowing how she'd be able to spend all night alone with Austin and not tell him everything she was thinking and feeling. The only thing keeping her from blurting it all out now was knowing it would hurt him to hear yet another girlfriend's view of what she wanted had changed because of a trip to see his family. Even if part of her knew he'd be proud that she was going after what she really wanted, the way he'd been each time she'd spoken up around Anais over the past few weeks. They had the fixed end date to the relationship already, so there was no need to give him details that would just make things painful for him.

"I'm sure." Austin wrapped his arm around Clementine. "You all have fun and say hello to the Hendersons for me."

There was a flurry of tidying up wrapping paper and gifts, then a round of air kisses for them both. Then they were alone. Just the two of them in an empty house with a roaring fire and beautiful Christmas decorations. It was like something from a movie, or from a dream.

Clementine couldn't stop shaking.

"You seem nervous." Austin came up behind her where she was standing in front of the fire and rubbed her arms.

She inhaled deeply and let her shoulders relax, then turned to smile up at him. "Just tired."

He frowned, a crease appearing in his perfect forehead while he smoothed back some of her hair from her face. "It has been a long week. Thank you again for coming."

"Austin, you don't have to thank me. I'm happy to be here. Your family is great."

He raised an eyebrow and she laughed.

"Really. I like them."

"They do seem to like you. I didn't even get a bag from Olivia, and she gave one to my parents' mailman."

Clementine looked around the room, taking in the splendor she still hadn't quite gotten used to. "It's a lovely place. Did one of your sisters decorate it for the holidays?"

Austin shook his head in a distracted sort of way and walked over to the tree. "No, it's a professional." He fiddled with an ornament. "I made this when I was a kid. I can't believe they kept it."

"You just said someone else did the decorating." Clementine came to stand next to him to see the little clay handprint painted with the letters of his name, the S backward.

"My parents bring a box of our ornaments wherever we're staying. The others have them too, but mine is always in the front. I don't know why. It's horrifically ugly."

Clementine chuckled. Even though he was brilliant, he didn't know everything.

"I think it's because they're very proud of you even if they don't always say it." She wrapped her arms around him, and he rested his chin on top of her head with a sigh.

"I wish I wanted the same things as they did sometimes," he mumbled into her hair. "It would make life so much easier."

"I know exactly what you mean." They were so similar in so many ways. Clementine shouldn't be surprised at how strong her feelings had gotten so quickly. Austin understood her in all the ways that no one else did, saw her in a way no one else ever had. Maybe... maybe there was a possible future where they could stay together. If she knew he was open to living somewhere else. "Is that why you moved to Colorado instead of doing a residency in California?"

"Clementine Miller, you know better than anyone how little choice residents get in where they go." The rumble of a laugh in his chest reverberated through her body and she closed her eyes, breathing him in and holding him tight. If they could just stay like this forever, wrapped in each other's arms in front of a roaring fire, then life would be perfect. "But to answer your question, no, I did not put any programs in California on my list."

A bright spot of hope buried itself in her chest.

"Though I did look for things close by. I do like being able to see them as much as I can. It's why I'm so grateful to Anais that I could come work with her when I wanted to leave my residency at CUH. I probably would have gone much farther away otherwise."

Deflated, Clementine pulled out of his warm embrace. So that was it then. There was no way he'd ever want to leave Jasper Creek. It was one of the things she liked best about him, that he loved his family, but it was this similarity between them that meant it wouldn't work.

"Can we not talk about my sister right now?" She wrinkled her nose and Austin laughed, shaking his head.

"What should we do instead?"

She looked around the room. The presents were all stacked in neat piles, and Austin had gotten some very nice ones from his parents. "Chess? And whiskey?"

Austin's eyes lit up. "You read my mind, Cutie."

"Just don't fall asleep before midnight, Dino, or I'll superglue your hand to your face."

"You wouldn't." His eyes narrowed as he pulled out the new marble chess set.

She helped him set it up on the floor in front of the fire. "Ask Dani if you don't believe me."

"I thought we weren't talking about your sisters."

"Do you want to hear the story or not?"

He got two glasses from a cabinet and poured them both two fingers of what Clementine knew must be very expensive whiskey. The first sip was smooth and warm and reminded her of kissing Austin. She flushed, and he grinned, wide and victorious.

"Of course I want to hear it." He settled himself in front of the board and moved a pawn two spaces forward. "Just try not to get distracted from the game. I won't be going easy on you just because you're cute."

"Don't bother. I was going to go easy on you because of your age."

He laughed and they settled into the game. They played and drank and talked well past midnight, sharing stories from their childhoods that were more similar than Clementine would have expected.

It would be hard when things ended with him in a few days, but it was better this way. They'd both be able to keep these memories of the time they spent together, and there'd be no messy breakup, no embarrassing admissions of feelings that the other didn't share, no hurt from reminders of past pain.

Clementine knew what she wanted now. She just wished Austin had wanted the same.

Christmas morning, he opened his eyes, and Clementine's dark eyes were staring right at him from where she lay at the edge of the bed, not blinking. It was as if she'd fallen asleep looking at him and hadn't wanted to miss anything all night.

"Good morning," he whispered, not sure if she was actually awake.

Her lips turned up. "Morning."

"Did you sleep well?"

"Like a rock. Dinner really wore me out."

"Just dinner? Or what came after?"

Her face flushed in the morning sunlight, her eyes sparkling. "All we did was talk."

"More than I ever have."

"You talk more than anybody I know, Dino."

"Not with women."

"Oh."

He could see these words sinking in, her mind processing all the meanings they could hold. It had been three perfect days, and today was Christmas. The other gift he'd gotten her was tucked into a pocket in his suitcase, and until last night, he hadn't been sure he'd even give it to her. But somewhere between his third glass of whiskey and her telling him a story about giving anchovy sandwiches to Dani and Eli and making them sick, he'd made the decision to tell her how he felt. The brush-off in the bathroom must have been her predinner nerves, and the only reason she was holding back had to be because she was worried he didn't feel the same. So he'd make it clear to her.

"I have something for you." He stood up, his blankets falling back onto the couch.

"What?" She sat up in bed, her face stricken. "I only got you that silly stuffie. I thought that's all we—"

"I wanted to do this. Don't worry about it."

"Should I be afraid?"

He didn't answer her. He didn't want to lie, didn't want this to be a joke. Instead of responding, he rummaged in his suitcase until he found the small box.

"It's just something small. When I saw it, I thought of you, that's all." He held out the box like it wasn't a big deal, but his heart was pounding, his pulse a raging river in his ears.

He was torn between wanting to observe her face carefully for every single reaction and wanting to look away and pretend he didn't care at all what she thought.

In the end, he settled somewhere in the middle, sitting back down on the couch, one hand resting on his knee, the other slung across the back. At ease. Confident. The image he'd given her this entire time, even when he was being the most vulnerable he'd ever been with her.

There was curiosity mixed with anxiety in her face, and her lip was firmly under her teeth as she opened the box. He had to look away, his chest was so full. The tiny gasp let him know she'd opened it.

"Austin, this is beautiful." He finally peeked at her, and she was holding up the dainty chain with the orange charm attached to it he'd spotted when out in the village earlier in the week. He could tell the moment she noticed that it was a clementine, because her eyes lit up brighter than the tree downstairs.

"It's a Cutie. Like you."

"Thank you." Her smile was wide as she pulled her legs under her on the bed. "Much better than all the Minnie Mouse stuff Bastien always gets me. I can actually wear this at work."

His heart sank down into his gut, past his knees, and all the way to the floor. The reminder of what was waiting for her back in Jasper Creek came at him in a rush, flattening him to the ground.

"You said Mark's not the guy you thought he was. Why?"

Her eyes shot up. "What are you talking about?"

"That's what you said when you asked if we could date for real." Austin forced his body to stay in his relaxed, confident pose on the couch, even as his chest felt like it might combust from the pressure of breathing normally. "What did he do?"

"Why does it matter?" She raised an eyebrow.

"Because I want to know that I was right."

The words burst out of him before he could stop them. The shock on Clementine's face was only temporary, quickly replaced by fury. It wasn't what he'd meant to say, even if it was what he needed to know. If he'd been wrong, at any point in this whole thing, then he might be wrong about how he thought she felt about him.

"Is that really all you care about?" It felt like she was miles away, though from her spot on the bed, they were barely ten feet apart.

"I care about you."

"Do you really?" Her voice was shaking. From anticipation because she felt the same or pity because she didn't?

He just didn't know, and it was making his brain squeeze tightly like there wasn't enough air in the room.

He leaned forward on the couch, head in his hands. It did nothing to relieve the pressure inside.

"Of course I do. But I didn't want you to think I expected anything from you, that I wanted anything to happen."

"But you do want something to happen?"

He threw up his hands. "I've wanted that for weeks."

The sharp gasp of her inhale was like a knife in his chest.

"And what about what I want?"

It wasn't him, is what she meant, but he'd keep pushing until she actually said the words.

"Do you know? Or are you waiting for someone to tell you?" He raked his hands through his hair. "Just decide, Clementine, and go for it. Stop looking for permission to do what you want."

"I hate it when people think they know what's best for me." Anger was starting to build, her face turning red and her expression closing off.

"I know you do."

"And yet you think you know better than me about this."

"That's not what…"

With an inhale that did nothing to slow his racing pulse or quiet his manic thoughts, he rubbed the back of his neck. He was at a loss, not for the first time with Clementine, but never had knowing the right thing to say been so important. This wasn't what he'd expected. He hadn't predicted she'd react this way. It was rare when he was wrong, but when he was, holy hell, did it hurt. Should he get up and go to her? Or stay on the couch and give her space? The weight of his uncertainty froze him in place, glued to his seat.

"I need to hear you say it. Whatever it is."

She threw herself out of bed, turned away to face the window and the snow-covered mountains that surrounded the house. The chain of the necklace was clutched in her fist, the clementine charm glowing in the morning light. "We agreed to break up after the trip."

His heart stopped, just for a moment but long enough to end him. "That's what you want?"

"Yes."

She was so certain, so sure, he couldn't help a burst of pride in the middle of his chest. It was what he wanted so much for her, even more than he wanted her to want him.

He took a deep breath. "We can do that, but..."

Part of him was still clinging to a last bit of hope. She still hadn't said the words. That she didn't want him. All he had to do was tell her how he really felt, say that he loved her, and see what happened. She'd surprised him enough times for him to not even think to expect to know what her reaction would be.

There was only one logical outcome, however, and it wouldn't be the happy ending Austin had been stupidly hoping.

"But what?" There was the smallest tendril of uncertainty in her voice, in her eyes, and all his resolve broke in an instant.

She was using him, just like Cassidy had, to get what she wanted. Except this time he'd asked for it. He'd willingly agreed to be her fake boyfriend, then her practice boyfriend, knowing the whole time she wasn't for him. So he wouldn't drag things out, wouldn't ignore the crystal clear messages that Austin's time with her was over. He wouldn't justify and rationalize and hold on as tight as he could until they were both so angry and frustrated that it all imploded in one terrible fight.

"But we should keep pretending so we don't give my family any drama to discuss once we leave. Then when we're back in Jasper Creek, we'll make a clean break."

Her eyes were full of something he couldn't quite describe. Halfway between pain and relief. "I don't know if I can do that. Can you tell them something happened with my family and I need to go home early?"

The words hit him so hard, right in the middle chest, he had to lean back on the couch to steady himself and take a deep breath before he could answer her.

"Of course."

What else could he do?

Of course he would let Clementine go. Without telling her how he really felt. He would let it be easy for her. He wouldn't muddy the waters with the same guilt and lingering loyalty that had kept Cassidy from making the clean break they'd needed.

Because a clean break was always best.

"Jackson refuses to play Bananagrams." This was the first thing Bastien said to her when he picked her up at the airport in Denver.

"Hello to you too." Clementine smiled as she got into his car. "Are you having a nice winter break?"

Bastien ignored her question and pulled out of the crowded pickup lane. "The teams aren't even, so we've been making Eli switch every round."

For the entire ride home, Bastien recounted each and every game that had been played while she was away and who had won. It was exactly what she thought would happen when she called her parents on Christmas afternoon to tell them she'd be coming home a few days early. Getting lost in the chaos of the Miller holidays was what she needed right now to distract her from the misery that had been clinging to her since her fight with Austin.

Since their breakup.

It wasn't supposed to feel like a breakup. That had been the deal. But nothing had gone the way she'd expected, ever since that first kiss on the top of her head in Carl's Café that felt like it had happened a million years ago.

"Hey, are you okay, Minnie?" Bastien paused in his blow-by-blow account of a particularly brutal round of charades that had somehow ended with a bloody nose for Jackson. Now his hesitancy to play Bananagrams made more sense. "You didn't catch whatever Austin's family got, did you?"

It had been the easiest way to explain her sudden return home from the trip. Austin would stay to take care of his parents and sisters while Clementine would head back to Colorado. What they'd told the Gibsons had been similar, but in reverse: everyone had caught the flu and she needed to head home to help out.

Lying to both of the families was uncomfortable, but the truth was so much more painful. She shifted in her seat and looked out the window at the snow-covered trees lining the highway. Her brother could read her face too well.

"Just feeling a little sick from the plane."

Clementine didn't think she could feel sicker than she had on the flight over, but going back on her own had been a thousand times worse. Before she got out of the car at the airport, Austin had handed her a bag of ginger chews. It made the airsickness much better, but the entire flight there had been a constant tug at her chest like her heart was being ripped in two.

Heartbreak actually hurts.

Bastien put a hand on her shoulder. "I can drop you off at your place instead of Mom and Dad's if you want."

"That would be nice, actually." Her heart squeezed in relief. It was good to be home with her family. "I want to check on Marbles and clean up a little before I head over."

And cry in her shower.

"Whatever you need, Minnie." Bastien turned off the highway at the exit for Jasper Creek. "You can tell us about your trip. I only saw that one picture you sent of the two of you at some party."

A posed shot, taken by Olivia after she gave Clementine instructions on how to angle her face, was what she'd sent her family at the beginning of the trip.

"I have more. Mostly of the mountains. And we have plenty of those here."

They were winding along the small road that led to Clementine's apartment, the mountains in question in full view.

"Still, I'd like to see them. I'd like to hear about your trip." He cleared his throat, his voice uncertain. "I hope Austin got you a nice present?"

Without thinking, her hand went to her neck, where she would have put the necklace, if she hadn't stuffed it in the bottom of her bag in the flurry of packing she'd done before leaving that morning. "Yeah, a stuffed cat like Jamie has. But it looks like Marbles."

"That's... sweet."

She finally turned to look at him and despite all the anguish swirling around in her chest, she had to laugh at how grumpy he looked. Like he'd been hoping that Austin had given her something terrible and he'd have a reason to be mad at him.

"Sorry to disappoint. He's a very good gift giver."

"Figures," Bastien mumbled as he pulled into the parking lot in her apartment complex. "You need help bringing in your suitcase?"

"I got it." She leaned over and gave him a quick peck on the cheek. Then she wrapped her arms around him. "I missed you."

He relaxed into the hug and gave her a quick squeeze back. "Missed you too, Minnie."

"I'll be over soon." She got out of the car, grabbed her bag from the trunk, then waved as he drove away.

Clementine had every intention of going over to her parents' house, but after her shower, she lay down for a minute and woke up six hours later with a headache and chills. The lie about illness cutting short the trip would have turned into the truth if she'd stayed in California another day.

Did she hate that her first instinct was to call Austin? Of

course. But he thought a clean break was best. He hadn't been wrong so far.

She could have asked her sister to come, but Anais would want to talk about the trip, and she wasn't ready to do that yet. She didn't think that she could pretend that she was still with Austin, even though it was what she'd have to do, at least for a few more days. From what he'd said in the car, Bastien was still wary of their relationship, and Anais was likely the same.

So she called her dad, who was there within ten minutes.

He was entirely focused on her health. Beyond checking if she'd had contact with anyone she knew to be sick, he didn't pry into the specifics. He gave her ibuprofen and made her soup. He cuddled next to her on the couch and showed her pictures. They were from the Miller family Christmas, the same ones Dani and Bastien had texted her, but she sat there and made the right sounds at the adorableness that was Jamie in various themed outfits—a Santa hat, reindeer ears, elf pajamas.

It was strange looking at the pictures and feeling both sadness at missing out but also delight that she'd had something entirely different. Even if her last day in California had been one of the worst of her life, she didn't regret going. She didn't regret seeing another way of doing things, another way of living. Though the glamorous, gossipy life the Gibsons lived was far from what she wanted for herself, it was the reminder that she'd needed. There were alternatives to the life the rest of her family had chosen in Jasper Creek. She wasn't sure she'd have gotten to that realization without everything she'd been through over the past few months with her fake—and then real, and now ex—boyfriend.

Thanks to Austin, the life she wanted seemed possible.

She just wished there could have been one with him in it too.

TWENTY-SEVEN
AUSTIN

The rest of the trip, in a word, sucked.

Luckily, the days between Christmas and New Year's Eve were so full of parties and dinners that it was easy for Austin to keep up the performance whenever he was around other people. Hayden wasn't the only good actor in the family after all.

So he repeated the line he'd practiced, telling the few people who asked—only those not completely self-absorbed had even noticed he'd had someone with him the previous week—that Clementine was fine, just needed to leave early because her parents had gotten sick. This got more than one confused look, but his own family understood.

"She was lovely, Austin," Olivia told him when she dropped him off at the airport after the loneliest, most miserable New Year's Eve he'd had in years. "Do whatever you can to make her happy. We want to see her again next year."

"I'm trying."

Though what could he do, now that she was back in Jasper Creek without him? When he'd dropped her at the airport with a bag of ginger chews, she'd said thank you, then walked away without looking back. She'd sent one text message to let him know she'd gotten home safely, and that was it.

That was harder than anything else really. To not know what she was thinking anymore, to not be able to share his thoughts.

If his family noticed his melancholy, they didn't say anything. That was the nice thing about them being a little too self-absorbed. It meant he could hide things easily.

But he knew he couldn't hold all this inside him forever. The second he was home, he drove to Gabby and Bastien's house, making a pit stop at Carl's.

It had been months since Austin had spent some time one-on-one with Gabby. Showing up unannounced at her house used to be okay, but now it took planning. Nap times, feeding schedules, unexpected sickness, something small could and had upset their plans countless times in the past few months.

Ignoring all of that, he showed up with hope in his heart that she'd be willing to see him.

And that Bastien would be out of the house.

"Austin!" She smiled wide when she opened the door, Jamie on one hip. "It's so nice to see you."

"Me or the donuts?" He held out the box from Carl's in his hand.

"Both." Eyes alight, she took his offering greedily and handed off her son to Austin.

He followed her inside and into the kitchen, Jamie babbling happily in his arms. Today the baby was particularly interested in his hair, grabbing fistfuls of it and pulling. Hard.

"I supposed I deserve that."

"What did you do?" Gabby asked through a mouthful of donuts.

"Is Bastien here?"

"At the gym with Jackson." Her eyes narrowed. "Why?"

"It's about Clementine."

Instantly, Gabby's eyes darkened. "Austin, I love you, but if you hurt that girl, I can't protect you from this family."

"Does no one really think she's capable of hurting me?"

"Is that what happened?"

"It's complicated." With a sigh, he put Jamie in the high chair next to the counter and took a donut for himself. "We weren't really dating. It was all to get the attention of the guy she's really into. But then she wanted to date for real, but not really, because it was just to practice for when she had a boyfriend and we were going to break up after the ski trip no matter what."

Gabby stared, open-mouthed, looking more surprised than she ever had. "You weren't really dating?"

"Not at first."

"But you two were so cute together."

"Yeah well. I'm from LA. We're all good at acting there." He bit into the donut. "My brother's Hayden Carmichael, by the way."

"He's what— No, don't even try to distract me right now." She held up a finger, which Jamie strained to reach. "What happened with Clementine? You caught feelings?"

He chewed his donut miserably, ignoring the way his chest was caving in. "Does that sound like something I'd do?"

"For such a smart guy, you can be spectacularly stupid some-times." Gabby shook her head.

Jamie gurgled in his high chair and sucked on his fingers. Austin made a face at the baby and Jamie giggled. "You know, he is the perfect mix of you and Bastien. The eyes are all you, but his nose is as Miller as could be."

"Stop changing the subject," Gabby said, then sat back down as if she'd realized something. "Though speaking of family resem-blances—"

"This has nothing to do with Hayden."

"Are you sure?" Gabby crossed her arms. "You just randomly picked today to finally tell me this major thing about you?"

"Yes." He stuffed the rest of the donut in his mouth. "Pure coincidence."

"Please chew before you choke. You're setting a bad example for my son."

He did as told, then made a face at her. "Knowing that means you'll understand why I was so good at all the acting I had to do for fake dating Clementine."

"Nothing about the two of you was fake."

"She just did it to get the attention of her boss, at least at first." Then to practice, because he wasn't what she really wanted.

"Who, Mark Vickers? He's been dating someone from Centennial U Hospital for months."

"What?" he said so loudly it upset Jamie, who began to wail. Though a crying baby was preferable to whatever was going on inside of him right now. Split between relief and fury, he didn't know if he should run out of there immediately to tell Clementine, or laugh at himself for how blind he'd been.

Gabby rolled her eyes and pulled her crying son out of his high chair. "Your mom mentioned it a few weeks ago? I think. I can't remember."

It didn't surprise Austin why Dr. Miller hadn't said anything to him. Hearing anything about CUH, even three years later, brought up bad memories, and he was careful never to ask. He leaned back and shook his head. "I am stupid, or I would have noticed ages ago and none of this would have happened."

"You see what you want to see."

"And what is that?"

"If you'd have noticed and told Clementine, she never would have agreed to fake date you."

"So you're saying I wanted Clementine this whole time and didn't know it?"

Rather than shoot right back with something quippy, Gabby tilted her head and considered Austin for a moment before answering. "No, I don't think so. You were in too much pain before to notice someone as nice as her."

Gabby wasn't wrong, but Austin had a rule about how many times he said that someone else was right in a year. He'd already said it once to Anais this year because she'd been right about Gabby's baby being a boy. He was saving the second time he said it for Clementine. He didn't know how or why he'd need it, but his hunches were almost always right.

In Mark's case, it was a rare example of him being wrong.

"So what changed, O wise and all-knowing Gabby?"

"Geez, I don't know, Austin. I'm not a genius. And my brain is still mostly mush thanks to this guy." She blew a raspberry on Jamie's belly, and the baby gurgled. "But if I had to make a guess, it's just one of those things. Situations change, timing is right. You can't always predict everything. Sometimes things just happen because they do."

This was the opposite of how he lived his life.

"If I can't predict it, then how can I be sure it'll work out?"

"You can't." She bounced Jamie on her knees. "You just have to roll with it. Did I expect to get pregnant three seconds after I married Bastien? Of course not."

"I could have told you that would happen."

She gave him a look, the one that let him know he was being obnoxious. She'd learned it from Anais. He could have sworn even baby Jamie looked at him askance. "You remember how freaked out I was about it, don't you?"

Austin nodded. "Of course."

Gabby had grown up completely differently from the Millers and the Gibsons. There'd been practically no parents at all. She'd taken care of her little sister, who had still chosen to cut her out of her life entirely. Falling for Bastien wasn't something she'd expected, but finding out she was pregnant when she'd never even imagined having kids of her own had been something else entirely. Austin remembered the anxious conversations they'd had at work, and his encouragement for her to seek out help from a mental health professional before making any decisions.

"Do you remember what you told me?"

"That you were strong enough and smart enough to figure it out."

She lifted a hand in the air and gave him a pointed look. "Gee, what good advice that might also possibly definitely apply here as well."

"This is totally different."

"You didn't expect to fall for Clementine though, did you?"

There wasn't a way to answer that where he didn't sound like either an asshole or an idiot.

"That's the thing about her. She keeps surprising me. I never know what to expect with her."

The smile that spread across Gabby's face was too smug for Austin's liking.

"So maybe you'll just have to wait and see what happens, rather than know in advance the way you do for everything else."

"That sounds like a terrible idea."

"I think it's the only option you've got."

"I could leave."

The gasp from Gabby was like a punch to the chest. "Leave?"

He ran his hands through his hair and down his neck. "I'm bored, Gabby. Maybe it's time for a fresh start somewhere else."

"You'd just pick up and leave, just like that?"

"A clean break is always best."

At this, Jamie started to cry for real, and no amount of shushing and rubbing of his back from Gabby could calm him down.

"Will you at least stay here while I go feed him?"

"Of course." Though he'd have been fine if she nursed there in the kitchen, he knew that for Gabby, having people around when feeding him distracted her and the baby.

She walked out, still shushing and rubbing, leaving Austin alone in the kitchen. He took a few minutes to tidy it up, brushing the donut crumbs from the counter and putting away the clean dishes in the dishwasher. It was soothing, the routine of cleaning, but also frustrating. It was like no matter what he did, there was always a mess to clean up.

The longer Gabby was gone, the more her words sank in. There wasn't really anything he could do other than wait. Clementine would eventually find out that Mark had a girlfriend, but since she no longer wanted him, it wouldn't make a difference in how she felt—or rather didn't feel—about Austin.

There was nothing he could do to change things, to move the chess pieces around in his favor. For all his scheming and machinations, his logical thinking and brilliant deductive reasoning, Clementine Miller would have to be the one to make the final move.

By the Monday morning after New Year's, Clementine was feeling better, whatever cold or flu having made its way through her system. She'd missed most of the festivities with her family, but they'd all either dropped in for a few minutes to check on her or given her a call every day. Coming home had been the right choice. Especially now that she was so determined to leave it behind sooner rather than later.

The heartbreak was still tender, but there was work to distract her. With her patients, she was chatty and polite as was expected, but she focused on asking them questions and letting them talk, rather than the typical back and forth she usually had with them. Whenever anyone asked how her holidays had been—and almost everyone asked—she said they'd been fine and turned the question back to the patient.

Because when someone asked that question, what they really wanted to do was tell you about theirs.

There was one person she probably should give some details to, but Mark had told everyone he'd be coming in late the first day back after the break, and she found herself grateful for it. She needed the time to process everything, to think about what she'd say, how she'd tell him.

Because a part of her didn't want to tell him. Part of her—a big part, if she was honest with herself, which she didn't really want to be right now—just wanted to be back in California with Austin.

It was lunchtime when Mark finally made an appearance, ducking into the break room to put a basket on the table.

"Hey, Clem. Have a nice holiday?"

"Yes, fine thanks." She took a deep breath. This was her chance to get started on the path she'd chosen over being stuck forever in Jasper Creek. She had to tell Mark everything. What she wanted for her career, her ideas for the clinic that didn't involve social media. Would it be relevant that things had ended with Austin? Maybe. "How was yours?"

"It was amazing." Mark had the biggest grin ever on his face as he leaned on the table where she was sitting. It was the same smile all her patients had that morning, the eager one that said he had a story he was bursting to tell.

"Oh yeah? What happened?" Her hands were suddenly clammy, and she smoothed them along her legs.

"I got engaged."

The air rushed out of her lungs. That had to mean the entire time she'd been trying to get his attention, he'd been dating someone. If she hadn't realized weeks ago where Mark's true interest in her lay, then she'd be devastated. Even so, it took a moment for her to find the breath to be able to say anything, and when she did, it was far from the right thing to say.

"Are you kidding?"

Mark's smile fell a little, and he took a step back. "No. Did I not mention I was seeing someone?"

He absolutely had never mentioned anything. Clementine plastered on a smile. "I must have forgotten. Was she with you at the Fall Festival? Or skiing?"

Mark shook his head. "She's in residency. Not a lot of time for weekend fun, unfortunately. But once she's done, we'll get married and everything will be great." His eyes were bright and his voice tender.

She'd never seen him look like this. This was what Mark looked like in love. How could she have ever thought the way he'd sometimes glanced at her had been anything like that?

Two of her colleagues came in, and Mark told them the news while Clementine sat motionless at the table like a plastic doll. Everyone else seemed much less surprised and a thousand times more enthusiastic in their congratulations.

How had she never heard he was dating someone? Austin must have known. Why not just tell her?

More of her colleagues came into the breakroom, and their excited chatter helped cover up Clementine's stunned silence.

Maybe Austin hadn't known. Maybe he just thought Mark was like every other guy who was jealous of Austin. It would be easier for Clementine to believe this than to admit to herself that she was a stupid girl with a crush who'd let that cloud everything... and make her agree to fake dating someone she never would have had dared consider as a possibility for her.

Finally, everyone else filed out of the room, leaving Clementine with her boss. Who, she now knew without a shadow of a doubt, had never been interested in her at all.

"Congratulations again." She said it with a smile that she wanted to mean, but couldn't quite just yet. This gave new flavor to the sneaky way he'd paid attention to her. Just enough so she'd think he was interested, all the while in love with someone else. Thank goodness she'd put aside her crush weeks ago.

That didn't mean it didn't hurt. She made her way to the door.

"Thanks, Clem. This will mean big changes for you."

She turned back at this, her head spinning. "I'm sorry?"

He came over and slapped her shoulder. "Once I'm married, I'll go back to living in Denver full time. I'll need someone to take over for me here."

There were no words. This was exactly what she wanted, the first step on the way to owning her own clinic, somewhere other than Jasper Creek. But it was too soon, too fast.

Too easy.

She leaned against the doorframe, unsteady on her feet. "Am I really the right person to do that? I haven't even been working a year."

"This clinic really took off when you joined." Mark tilted his head and scrunched up his nose. "That silly social media idea showed me you care about this place. But you won't need to do any of that. Just be yourself. Clementine Miller, DPT."

Had this been his plan all along?

Taking a deep breath, she asked the question she should have asked weeks ago. Personal disappointments aside, he was still her boss. This was still her job, and she wanted to be good at it. "Did you only hire me because of my family?"

He ran a hand along the back of his neck and looked down. "Look, it's what got you the interview, but you've proven yourself." His eyes met hers, and he gave her a shrug and a half smile. "And it's proven useful to have you here. You should be proud the town loves you so much. It'll mean great things for your career."

The truth hit her square in the chest, hard enough to make her vision blur and her ears ring. There was a tickle from the chain dangling around her neck, and she brought a hand up to the clementine charm, rubbing her fingers against it.

She'd been a complete idiot.

"Can I think about it?" Her voice was trembling, and she leaned hard into the doorframe, the comfort of its solidity reassuring her she wasn't dreaming this entire weird conversation.

"Um, I guess?" Mark frowned and scratched at the three days of scruff on his chin. Had he always been this unkempt, or had she just never noticed before? "I mean, there's time to talk. I won't get married until next year—"

"Great. We'll talk soon."

Running from the room before she burst into tears in front of the last person who'd care if she did, she escaped to the one place Mark wouldn't find her: the women's bathroom.

Less than a minute into her sobfest, however, someone else came in. She looked up, wiping her eyes, and saw her colleague Melissa looking at her with wide eyes and an open mouth.

"Clem, are you okay?"

"Um, yeah." She bit the inside of her cheek. Not saying what she really meant had gotten her into this mess. "Actually, no, I'm not. And I kind of hate being called Clem."

"Oh, I'm sorry, Clementine, about the nickname. I didn't know." Melissa put a sympathetic hand on her shoulder, the same one her boss had slapped collegially before turning her whole world upside down. "Is that why you're crying?"

She shook her head. "I broke up with Austin over the holidays." Though she was still wearing the necklace he'd given her, out of some masochistic stubbornness. She'd told him she'd wear it at work, so she had.

"That's awful, sweetie." She grabbed a tissue from the box on the counter and handed it to her. "I guess Mark was right."

Clementine wiped her nose and sniffed. "What do you mean?"

"He's never liked Dr. Gibson. Apparently, he hooked up with his sister when she was here a few years ago and never called her back."

For the second time in less than an hour, Clementine felt like a ton of bricks had hit her. "Mark told you this?"

Melissa nodded. "He would grumble about it all the time when you weren't around. I think he didn't want to say anything to you though. It wasn't really his place."

But he had said enough to let her know he expected Austin to break her heart. Mark had also antagonized him, battled with him, making it clear he hated Austin and was concerned for Clementine.

Concerned, but not interested. Not romantically. Only interested in keeping her here, in making sure she didn't leave, heartbroken, and put his clinic at risk.

"It wouldn't have made a difference anyway. Like I said, I broke up with him."

"Okay..." Melissa frowned like she didn't believe her.

"Things were getting too serious, and I'm not sure if I'm ready for that." Not that this was any of Melissa's business, but at least it wiped the incredulous look off her face.

Mark must have taken Clementine spending the holidays with Austin's family as a sign things were headed in a good direction. That he could take the risk and propose to his girlfriend.

Clementine wiped her face and looked in the mirror at her puffy red eyes.

Had Mark known about her crush on him?

Of course he had. He was a smart man. Just like Austin, who'd tried to tell her Mark wasn't interested in her in subtle ways, but she'd been too blind to notice.

What else had she been too blind to see?

Somehow, she made it through the rest of the day, her emotions strung tight as a telephone wire and just as electric. It took almost no effort at all to keep her eyes averted from Mark's office door. Her attention was entirely on her patients, but in the five minutes between appointments, her brain was flipping through options about what she should do next.

Her first instinct was to talk to Austin.

Not because he'd tell her what to do but because he'd tell her that she already knew. And then he'd make her squirm until she said it out loud.

Austin was not exactly an impartial party in this, however, so the second work was over, she raced over to Bastien and Gabby's house.

She knocked on the door, not sure if she'd rather see her brother or his wife. While it would be awkward to talk about guys to her brother, his dislike for Austin would be a good balance, and he'd remind her of the reasons to not be with him. On the other hand, talking to Gabby would be nice since she was friends with Austin and not in the family. An outsider's perspective on the situation was just what she needed.

She'd never considered there would be a third option, that Austin would open the door, her nephew in his arms.

"What are you doing here, Cutie?" Austin inhaled sharply, the cold winter air hitting his lungs so hard he took a step back. That nickname wasn't appropriate anymore. Clean break. "Sorry. Clementine."

It was just wishful thinking on his part that her eyes seemed to dim at that.

"Can I come in?"

"Sure." He stepped back, and Jamie cooed, reaching his hands out to Clementine. She took him without a word, and the simplicity of it—her taking a baby out of his arms, like she'd done it a hundred times, like this was what happened every evening after work—was enough to make his chest cave in.

"Where are Bastien and Gabby?"

"Out to dinner." He followed her into the living room, where she sat on the couch and balanced her nephew on her knees while she took off her coat and put it next to her. Then she picked up the book Austin had been reading to Jamie.

"Did she go back to work already?" Her eyes were on the baby, in what could have been extreme attentiveness, or as a way to avoid looking at him. Or both.

He moved to sit in the chair across from her, blood rushing through his ears.

"Next week."

"Huh." Clementine paged through the book, pointing things out to her nephew with wide, exaggerated facial expressions. Were her eyes redder than usual? Had she been crying? "Three months went by really fast."

"Did you come here to discuss Miller Family Medical's parental leave policy or for something else?" There was an exaggerated casualness to his words that she didn't seem to notice. Nor did she appear to pick up on the way his hands had closed into tight fists at his sides.

It had been three long days of waiting and wondering. She'd been to work today, since she was in the terrible olive-green uniform. Had she talked to Mark? Jealousy surged in his chest, even if Austin knew Clementine no longer wanted her boss. But there was always the possibility something had changed. After all, as Gabby had so generously pointed out, Austin couldn't predict everything. So while he was reasonably sure he knew why Clementine was here, not knowing if he was right sent his pulse into overdrive.

And then he noticed the necklace, sending sparkling orange light across Jamie's face.

"I found out why Mark hates you." Her eyes were still on Jamie and the book, so she didn't see how Austin clutched the arms of his chair at this.

"Besides the fact I'm smarter and more attractive than he is?"

"How would he know you're smarter— No, never mind, not important." She took a deep breath and looked up, then scrunched up her face like she was giving him bad news. "Apparently, you hooked up with his sister a few years ago when she was in Jasper Creek. And didn't call her."

"That... sounds like me." Disappointment rippled through him. His past had never seemed to matter to Clementine, but for her to bring it up now felt like a closing door. The necklace must not mean what he thought it did.

"It's not though." Clementine was shaking her head, Jamie mimicking her with uncoordinated movements.

"Thank you for that, but you don't know what I was like back then. You only saw me at work." Despite his prodigious memory, it was impossible for him to remember every single woman he'd been with. Especially in those first months in town, his heart so shattered he could barely get out of bed most days. "Will it make him feel better to know I never called anyone back?"

Her lips curved up. "Probably not." She set Jamie down in his playpen, then gave him a few toys. "He's not thinking about that right now though. He just got engaged."

The slow inhale kept his heart from beating itself out of his chest, but it also kept him from saying the first thing that popped into his mind. The air was suddenly lighter, and the world was coming into focus again. He slung an arm over his chair and raised an eyebrow.

"Did he?" he said after a moment.

"Uh-huh."

"Interesting."

Her face was a blank canvas, and he knew whatever came next would surprise him. It could be good, or bad, but either way, it would be unexpected. He braced for heartache.

"He also said he's going to have me take over the clinic after he gets married."

Her eyes met his, and the air stilled around them.

Austin licked his lips and stopped himself from congratulating her, from assuming he knew what she was thinking or feeling. "Is that what you want?"

"No." She sat back and, with an arm over the back of the couch, mirrored his casual posture.

"Really?"

"You sound surprised."

"I don't know everything, Cu—Clementine."

Her eyes widened, the surprise as visible on her face as if she'd cried out.

"I do want to run my own clinic one day, just..." Folding in on herself, she pulled her arm off the back of the couch and looked down at her hands, twisting them in her lap. All of his muscles were aching to reach out to her, but he held back.

"Not in Jasper Creek," he said softly. Suddenly it all clicked into place and his heart sped up so much it was a struggle to keep his words even. "Were you worried that I'd be keeping you here, since I'll be taking on more at the clinic now that Anais and Jackson are expecting?"

"As usual, you're right." Shaking her head, she rolled her eyes. "Everything would have been so much easier if I hadn't fallen in love with you."

Her final words were drowned out by Jamie's irritated squeal. Surely trained by his father to make Austin's life as difficult as possible, the baby had batted a toy out of the playpen.

Heart pounding, Austin bent to pick up the toy and hand it back to Jamie. It took another breathless moment before he lifted his face to meet Clementine's dark gaze. "Say it again."

She shifted on the couch and bit her lip, but her eyes never left his. "I love you."

"Not that." He leaned forward, a smile curling the edges of his mouth. "As I recall, someone once claimed she'd never say certain words regarding how correct I am that I believe I just heard."

She narrowed her eyes. "I'm not saying it again. It was a onetime thing."

"Forever is a long time. I'm sure it'll happen at some point."

"Forever? Someone sounds pretty confident considering you haven't asked me anything and I have agreed to nothing." She crossed her arms and leaned back.

He chuckled and stood up, making his way around the playpen to sit next to her on the couch. In the next heartbeat, she was in his arms and he was burying his face in her hair. It was the inky black of a bottomless ocean. "I love you so much."

From the depths of his embrace, she snuggled in closer and his heart squeezed tight. "I know."

"Do you want to move to Wyoming with me?" The words came from some deep corner of his brain, the part that wanted something, anything new, and he wanted it with her, immediately.

"No."

"No?" He pulled out of the hug to look at her. Once again, she'd surprised him. His mouth spread into a smile that felt like it would stay there forever.

Scooching away from him, she lifted her chin, eyes determined. "You're moving to New York with me."

"I am, am I?" The goofy grin he knew he had on his face must look ridiculous, and he didn't care at all. "You sound pretty confident considering you haven't even asked me, Cutie."

"I want to be with you, Dino, wherever that is. You make me feel like I can do anything."

"And you are the most interesting, surprising person I know."

"So will you come to New York with me?"

The word yes was on the tip of his tongue, but he had to make sure. "Could you really handle being that far from your family?" He looked down at Jamie, who was kicking a toy with his legs like there was nothing at all emotionally earth-shattering happening around him.

She wrapped her arms around him and stared up at him, a secret smile tugging the edges of her lips he was about two seconds away from kissing off her face. "I wouldn't be that far from family. I'd have you."

There were no words to answer that, so he did his best to show her with his mouth, his hands, his heart. It was entirely possible they'd have stayed on that couch all afternoon if not for a very noisy baby who demanded attention after barely any time at all had passed.

Jamie had definitely been trained by Bastien.

"I'll go," Austin said as Clementine picked up her nephew and set him on her knees. "On one condition."

Smoothing down Jamie's hair as he made a grab for her necklace, she raised a single eyebrow.

He leaned forward and gave her a quick kiss. "You have to be the one to tell Anais."

She inhaled slowly, eyes wide, then nodded. "Deal." A wicked smile pulled Clementine's perfectly kissed mouth wide. "But you'll be the one to tell Bastien."

EPILOGUE

"Hi, I'm Clementine."

No, that wasn't right. Clementine shook her head. Her smile was too big and you couldn't hear the words clearly.

"I'm Clementine Miller, DPT." Pause, then smile. "At Harmony Physical Therapy, we believe—"

"Do you want a bagel?"

"Austin!" Clementine whirled around to face her boyfriend, who was grinning like he knew exactly what he'd interrupted. "I need to practice. We're filming today."

He leaned against the open door as Marbles made his way between his legs. "You've been practicing all week, Cutie."

Turning back to the mirror, she frowned at her reflection. "I'm just nervous."

Austin came up behind her and wrapped his arms around her. The tiny Brooklyn bathroom was half the size of the one she'd had back in Jasper Creek, and with the two of them filling the entire space, they could barely move. The same thing happened in the minuscule kitchen and the microscopic living room.

Clementine had never been happier.

"I know you are." Austin planted a kiss on top of her forehead. "So why don't we get bagels and eat them on 'our' bench before you head into work?"

Around the corner was a park where they'd eaten their first meal after moving to New York and discovering the furnished apartment they'd rented was not, in fact, furnished. Between job hunting, them both getting licensed in the state, finding a place to live, and saying all of their goodbyes, the move had taken months of planning and preparation. It was inevitable that something would go wrong, and—as she reminded him almost daily—Austin couldn't predict everything.

But he knew her well enough to predict what she'd need that morning.

"Can we get some for everyone at the clinic too?" She met his eyes in the mirror and he grinned.

"Of course."

The practice she'd joined was huge, with over a dozen locations. Clementine was at the largest, with over a dozen therapists, as well as the corporate office. Within weeks after arriving and expressing her interest in the social media side of things, they had her filming videos at each of their clinics almost weekly. Now she was working on a series of recruitment videos, because they were expanding as fast as they could to keep up with demand.

She was learning more than she'd ever thought possible and was loving every minute.

Then she'd come home to Austin cooking dinner and fall in love with her life in New York all over again.

"I'll feed Marbles, then we can go, okay?" Austin gave her head another kiss and walked out of the bathroom with the cat following close behind. "Should we pick some up for your brother as well?"

"I don't know what time his interview finishes." With a final check of her hair and makeup, Clementine stepped into the small hallway and grabbed her jacket. "We can take him some tomorrow morning."

Eli was in New York for med school interviews, and Clementine was hoping he'd end up in the city as well. With two of them there, then maybe their other siblings would visit. Though it was easier for Clementine and Austin to head back west since getting a cat sitter was easier than traveling with multiple toddlers.

"Speaking of brothers," she said when Austin joined her in the hallway. "I thought I saw Charlie the other day and waved at him, but he ignored me."

"It wasn't him. He's in Sweden filming." Austin shook his head and slipped on his jacket, his arm bumping into Clementine and then the wall. "It was probably his look-alike."

"I'm sorry, what?" She froze with her own jacket halfway on.

"Yeah, there's a guy who looks just like him who lives in the city. Charlie hires him sometimes to fool the press when he's in town and doesn't want to be bothered."

"The new things I learn about your family..." Shaking her head, she followed him outside, where they were immediately hit with the hustle and noise of the city. It was busy on their little side street for a Tuesday, but she was happy to have an excuse to squeeze closer to Austin as they walked.

"That's nothing." He wrapped an arm around her shoulder and guided her down the street toward the bakery. "Did I ever tell you about my dad's uncle, who dated Marilyn Monroe before she was famous?"

As the crowd swallowed them up, Clementine leaned into Austin, listening closely and breathing him in deeply. Whatever he wanted to tell her, she was happy to hear. She was with the man of her dreams in the city of her dreams, and it was nothing like she'd ever imagined it would be.

It was better.

CURIOUS ABOUT HAYDEN CARMICHAEL?

Austin's little brother is featured in another sweet romance I've written, Man Of My Dreams.

Keep reading for a sneak peek!

Chapter 1

You dream it, and I'll make it happen . . .

The familiar words, spoken so close to her ear, pulled Bree out of a deep sleep. Looking around the room, her heart pounded in her chest.

Where was she?

Instead of familiar venetian blinds and small windows, there were large panes of glass covered in frothy pink curtains that let in an enormous amount of light. Too much light for this time of day.

A few blinks cleared the fog, and she flopped back into the unfamiliar bed. The scent of mothballs invaded her nose.

She was in Aunt Agatha's New York City apartment. Bree's apartment now.

Bree wiped away the tear that trickled down her cheek and sat up again. Her laptop was still open on the bed, where she'd fallen asleep watching *Escape to New York*. The voice that had woken her up was Hayden Carmichael's during one of her favorite, swooniest parts in the movie.

The superstar's first big hit was almost twenty years old, but it was what had planted the seed of moving to the city in her middle school brain. That seed had grown over the years into a dream, a massive bundle of desire like one of those gigantic topiary house-plants that took over an entire bookshelf with its tendrils and twists.

With a yawn, she closed her laptop with the movie still play-ing, then stretched slowly as she looked around the room. She'd barely taken it all in last night when she'd arrived, exhausted after two delayed flights and a very expensive cab ride she was sure should have cost at least half as much as she'd been charged. Between her Minnesota accent and her wide-eyed exclamation of joy at seeing the Statue of Liberty, the cab driver had assumed she was a tourist.

Except thanks to Agatha, Bree's first trip to New York wasn't as a tourist, but as a resident. A grin spread across her face. This was the first day of the life she'd always dreamed of.

Sleep still clung to the edges of Bree's eyes, and she rubbed them while stifling another yawn. She needed coffee. Immediately. Then she'd head out into the city.

Though dulled by her exhaustion, excitement was making its way through her system. She wrapped herself in her worn terry cloth robe and slipped on the new sheep's wool slippers she'd splurged on at the airport.

She stood up, and her shins banged into the night table. She turned, banged her knee on the bed, then tripped over her suitcases that were still piled in a heap, wedged in between the bed and the wall.

The smile slipped from her face as she half climbed, half

limped out into the hallway. The bedroom had seemed enormous last night in her half-conscious state of mind, but in the morning light, it was tiny.

Stumbling over creaking floorboards, she walked five steps into the kitchen. It was just as small, and even worse . . .

"Where's the coffee?" she asked the empty room.

Bree hadn't gone without some form of caffeine in her body within minutes of waking for over fifteen years. One of the perks of being a barista for as long as she had was that she knew how to make a good cup, no matter what she had on hand. Instant, whole beans, whatever kind of milk was available. Big cups, small cups, no cups. She could make anything work.

No coffee at all, however, made it impossible to even get started. A frantic search through the cupboards and drawers confirmed that, unless she wanted to make her morning cup out of mouse droppings and dead roaches, she was out of luck.

Did Birdbrain Bree forget to bring any food to an apartment that's been empty for forty years?

The mocking voices echoed in her ears as Bree took a few steadying breaths. She reminded herself that her forgetfulness was what Aunt Agatha had loved most about her. It was even in the letter accompanying the surprising announcement from Agatha's lawyer that she'd left Bree a Manhattan apartment in her will.

To my darling Bree, with a heart full of dreams and her head in the clouds, I hope this leads you to your happily ever after.

"No coffee." She closed a dusty cupboard and tightened the belt on her robe. Sunlight and the sound of honking horns filtered in through the kitchen window. "That's fine. Plenty of coffee in New York."

If her best friend, Leigh, were here, she'd look up the closest and best-rated café in the area. Bree was much happier to wander around and see what she could find. It always yielded the most interesting results. Bree trusted fate way more than Google for these kinds of things.

Before she could let fate do her thing, however, she had to get dressed. Leggings and a tank top might have been okay for a quick run to the store back home, but this was New York City. She could be anyone she wanted to be here. It was her chance to reinvent herself.

She dragged one of her suitcases into the living room, bumping into the couch and the coffee table. Heat was starting to pool under her arms. She took a quick sniff. Did she have time for a shower?

No, coffee was more important. Whatever she pulled out first, she'd wear. She'd only brought her favorite clothes with her and sold the rest, along with her car. With a little luck, she'd have enough funds for a few months before she'd need to worry about finding a job.

As if to make up for the lack of coffee, the most perfect sundress fell right into her hands the second she opened her suitcase. A smile lifted the corners of her mouth, her shoulders dropped, and her body relaxed. It would be okay. This was the perfect dress for what would be the most perfect first day of her new life.

Ten minutes later, she was putting on a pair of strappy sandals when she heard a thump from the hallway. A stream of curses followed. It sounded like an old woman. Like Aunt Agatha. Bree's shoes clicked as she went to the door and peered out the peephole.

It *was* an old woman, cursing up a storm. Her papery-thin white skin was deeply lined. She'd dropped what looked like an entire library's worth of books and was bending slowly to pick them up, one by one, to replace them in her overturned shopping caddy.

Bree didn't even hesitate. This was clearly someone meant to be in Bree's life.

After opening the door, Bree stuck her head out into the hallway. "Hi there, looks like you could use some help."

The old woman turned to look at her and raised an eyebrow. "Ya think?" She turned back to her books.

A real New Yorker, Bree thought with an excited quiver in her stomach. The old woman was a bundle of mismatched clothing. Green knitted leggings peeked out from below a long purple skirt. A light-gray puffy jacket was zipped up tight. It seemed like an odd combination for mid-May, but older people were often colder than others.

Bree stepped into the hallway and bent to pick up a few books. It wasn't that easy with the sundress, which turned out to be shorter than she'd remembered, and the sandals were hard to balance on. This was more of an outfit to be seen in than to help people in.

The woman didn't say anything but did grunt a bit when Bree managed to totter over and place a few books into her caddy.

"I just moved in."

Another grunt.

"It was owned by my aunt." Bree tucked the hair that had escaped her braid behind her ear. "Well, not really my aunt, but someone I knew my whole life who taught dance in my town, and I would go there after school and—"

She clammed up when the old woman paused and peered closely at Bree. Without a word, she went back to the books. There were only a few left now, and it took Bree a single unsteady swoop of her arms to gather them up and dump them on top of the rest.

It was a staggering amount of books, really, and Bree wasn't sure how the old woman planned on getting them all downstairs. They were only on the second floor, but there were at least twenty stairs. Last night they'd felt like a million, lugging her suitcases behind her at midnight.

"Do you need some help down the stairs?"

With a silent eye roll at Bree, the old woman pulled her cart down the other end of the hall, toward a gilded doorway Bree hadn't noticed. Smiling smugly, the old woman opened the door and stepped into an elevator. The clanking of the machinery was earsplitting, but it still would have been preferable to banging her suitcases up the stairs last night.

Hypnotized by the slowly fading elevator noises, Bree shook her head.

The old woman hadn't talked to her at all. Not even a hello, never mind about asking her name. Back home, that would have been the height of rudeness.

New York is home now. The smile slipped back onto her face.

Brushing off her skirt, Bree turned back to her door to retrieve her keys and phone before heading out into the city.

The handle wouldn't turn.

With her pulse pounding in her ears and sweat on her palms, she tried to open the door again, knowing before she even touched it what the outcome would be.

She was locked out.

A familiar flutter made its way up her chest. This was clearly a sign to explore, to discover the city in the spontaneous way she knew would lead to amazing things the way things like this always did.

Thanks to her restless spirit and taste for adventure, Bree had traveled all over the country, where she'd met endlessly fascinating people, collecting their stories while waiting for her own to start. Now it finally was, and she wasn't about to let getting locked out of her minuscule apartment ruin her perfect first day.

The elevator clanged from the back of the hallway, drawing her eye. If all her neighbors were like the old woman, Bree would have better luck getting someone in the street to help her call the building's super.

Without wasting another moment, she walked down the stairs and out the door to see what her new city had in store for her.

The tree-dappled street her apartment building was on led to a wide avenue with a familiar name. Seeing the "Broadway" street sign brought to mind theater marquees and neon lights, but here it was all bright awnings and graffitied trucks. The beep of car horns mingled with the chatter of pedestrians. Words in languages other than English mingled with the unfamiliar and delicious smells that wafted out food carts and open doors.

Dodging people and telephone poles, she weaved in and out of the crowd, taking in every new sight, every new sound. The buzz of far-off construction floated on top of everything.

"Holy cow." Bree had never seen so many people before. It was almost enough to make her remember that she was phone-less and wallet-less.

It was also chillier than she'd expected, but she was from Minnesota. All the shivering her body insisted on was because of her excitement, not the cold.

At least now the old lady's warm clothes made sense. Bree's floaty sundress gave her about as much protection from the biting wind as tissue paper. Several people she walked past gave her slightly raised eyebrows beneath their hoods and hats protecting them against the unseasonably cold May weather.

Ignore them. Just like she did back home whenever her unusual outfits clashed with everyone's small-town sensibilities. Minnesota Bree was flighty and flaky and forgetful. "Birdbrain Bree," as her family liked to call her with a chuckle. She, of course, always laughed along, clinging to whatever unique identity they wanted to pin on her. It was better than not being thought of at all.

New York Bree would be different. She shook back her hair and puffed out her chest, determined to walk in the confident, catwalk stride like people in the movies as they moved along busy New York sidewalks.

Holding each person's eye gave her a small thrill, a sense that despite the rocky start, her dream New York life—her dream New York self—was totally possible. Nothing bad happened when she made eye contact with people, except she almost ran into a few others going the opposite way. Even so, no one shouted at her, and a few people even smiled.

Smiled! Sure, they could have been laughing at her poor wardrobe planning, but through her optimistic eyes, they were all smiles of welcome.

After a few blocks, however, an unfamiliar, uncomfortable heaviness settled in her chest. Her stomach gave a growl loud enough that a dog barked at her from the backpack he was being carried in.

Her eyes flitted from one storefront to another. A gym, a shipping store, clothing for dogs, shoes for humans, a grocery store that took up half a block . . . She should go into one and explain her situation, but which one? It must happen all the time, people losing their phone.

If things got very desperate, she could always go to a police station. Someone in this teeming mass must know if there was a police station inside one of these white-stoned buildings. Someone would help her.

Her attention shifted back to the people streaming past her on the sidewalk. Everyone looked so serious, on their way to work or school, sipping from to-go cups of coffee that Bree tried not to salivate over. Back home, she'd have known at least half the faces and they'd have all gladly helped her.

Except some of the people streaming by did look familiar. Not in a super famous way, more like in a social media influencer way. Like they were all professionally good looking and were paid a lot of money to look that perfect all the time.

Hayden Carmichael lives in New York. The cold left her body, and heat crept up her neck. It was just like the movie she'd been watching last night. A girl, new to the city, bumps into him. He spills his drink all over her new dress . . .

Bree shook her head. The lack of coffee was making her light-headed. It was a city of eight million people. Even if he did live in her neighborhood, which she had no way of knowing, that only narrowed things down by a few million. Out here on the sidewalk, Bree had literally never seen so many people in her entire life.

Except, suddenly, there he was, walking toward her.

The shock of it made her stumble. Shivering as she straightened, she blinked and focused her gaze on him, trying to ignore the pounding of her heart in her ears.

Dressed in gym shorts and a hoodie, Hayden Carmichael's short hair was wet like he'd just showered. His eyes were partially blocked behind round glasses, but there was no mistaking that face, that scruff, those cheekbones. That perfect pout of a mouth that was tugged down in a concentrated frown instead of the wide grin he was usually photographed with, no matter what he was doing.

Bree stopped for a moment, stumbling again when someone plowed into her from behind and cursed at her. Afraid to take her eyes off him, she let her head swivel, looking back. Her heart almost stopped when his head turned, he looked back at her, and their eyes locked.

Was Hayden Carmichael *staring at her?*

A gasp got caught in her throat. This was absolutely the most perfect day.

Letting out her breath in a sigh, Bree picked up her pace, nearly skipping in delight.

I can't wait to tell Leigh what happened. She'd never believe it. Bree turned her head to look in front of her again, just in time to see a door swing open and to run smack into it.

Everything went black.

Chapter 2

Aiden was used to the stares. Through no fault of his own, his face was famous, even if he wasn't. Most days, in the midst of his familiar routine—gym, clients, animal shelter, studying—he didn't even notice the stares.

Did he occasionally stare back? Of course. New York was full of beautiful people. If they wanted to look at him, he'd enjoy returning the favor.

Things never went past looking, however. It took people all of two minutes with him to realize he wasn't the movie star they thought he was. When women gave him the googly heart-eyes the way this one was, he would hold their gaze for a moment, let them wonder, then go on with his day.

Today, however, he looked again.

There was an aura of pure sweetness radiating from her, like she was a fairy who'd stepped out of an enchanted forest and had no idea how she'd ended up in New York. Her long, dark hair and bright-blue eyes hinted at both mischief and warmth. She was impossibly beautiful and improbably dressed.

When Aiden turned his head for another look, a frown tugged at his lips. Was she shivering? Had she not checked the weather before leaving the house in that tiny dress?

Their eyes met again, and time slowed, Aiden's heart beating a staccato rhythm he hadn't felt since those early days in the city a decade ago. His heart stopped entirely when her face smashed into a door neither of them had noticed.

A curse flew out of his mouth that earned him a few more stares.

Before the woman's head had even hit the pavement, Aiden was at her side.

His hand found her pulse the way he'd been trained to do, and he was careful not to touch her or move her in case anything had been hurt that he couldn't see. His stomach gave a lurch when he considered just what kind of injuries she might have.

She was lying on the sidewalk like an extra in a superhero movie who'd been tossed to the side by the bad guy. Without hesitation, he stripped off his hoodie and laid it over her, thankful he'd been on his way to the gym and not on his way home, so it smelled like fabric softener, not sweat.

"Is she okay?" someone asked. A crowd had started to gather behind him, but he paid them no attention and focused on handling the situation in front of him.

Taking a deep breath, he went through the mental checklist of what to do when someone hit their head. She was breathing, and there was no blood. Next, he should see if he could wake her up.

"Miss? Can you hear me?"

There was a flutter of eyelids and a sharp intake of breath that had his pulse racing. Her blue irises were edged in black, and they were now looking up at him with that same intense gaze from before she fell.

"I had a dream about you." Her voice was strong, and loud.

There was a tittering of laughter behind him. Aiden ignored them and the drop in his stomach, staying focused on the woman.

"Oh yeah? What was I doing?" Keeping her talking was good. Head injuries were serious things, and he'd seen quite a few in the various jobs he'd had. Though he felt more confident treating animals than humans, he had the treatment steps memorized for both.

She blushed. "I don't remember."

Her blush suggested otherwise, but it also meant she was reacting relatively normally. He checked his watch, quickly updating his schedule for the day. Just a bit longer. Then he'd have to be on his way, or he'd be late. "What's your name?"

"Bree."

"Brie? Like the cheese? Or is that short for something?"

"I'm not cheese." She frowned.

Despite the tension in his chest, he let out a small chuckle at how vehement her answer was, the lilt of a midwestern accent turning the irritated words into a song.

She shifted slightly beneath his hoodie. "It's short for something, but I'm not sure what. Everyone just calls me Bree."

Uh-oh. Memory loss was never a good sign.

"Bridget?" He guessed.

Another frown and his breath hitched. The puckered skin between her eyes was inexplicably adorable.

Her blue eyes blinked up at him, a little too bright. "You look really familiar. Do I know you?"

Aiden hesitated. She did, but not in the way she thought she did. "You've never met me. I would have remembered someone like you."

She flushed again at this, and he cursed his unexpected candor. Unplanned words didn't often leave his mouth. He got back to his head trauma first-aid checklist.

"Does anything hurt?"

"Um . . . my head." She reached up to touch the rising bump on her forehead and winced.

He gently pulled her hand away, ignoring the tingling in his fingers at the feel of her skin on his. "You fell. It'll hurt for a while. Anything else?"

She shook her head, then her face tightened, and she groaned.

"Don't move, just say the words. Are you sure nothing else hurts?"

"No."

"Can you wiggle your fingers and toes?"

"You said not to move."

Aiden's heart thudded at the slight teasing edge to her voice and the small quirk of her lips.

There were murmurs and movement behind them, and Aiden glanced over his shoulder. The crowd was dispersing, apparently convinced he had it under control. One man hung back, however, and squatted down next to them.

"Should she go to a hospital?" His silvery eyebrows drew together. "That fall looked pretty nasty. And she can't remember anything."

"No hospitals." Bree sat up. Aiden's hoodie dropped away, and her dark hair fell down her back in a tangle of wild waves and half-done braids. She shivered.

An attentive ache rushed through him, and Aiden draped his hoodie around her shoulders again. "Why no hospitals?"

Bree looked around and frowned, pulling the hoodie tight against her body. "I don't know."

"That's okay. At least you remember your name."

A corner of her lip turned up. "Only part of it."

Oh hell, she was too cute for her own good. Every protective instinct inside of Aiden was on fire in a way they hadn't been in a long time. Maybe it was the way her hair fanned out around her head, wispy and cloudlike. Or the way her accent brought to mind wholesome images like cornfields and crystal-clear lakes that were incongruous to the dirty, smelly city that surrounded them.

The city that had literally just knocked her on her ass.

"Can you remember where you live?" It was the other man who spoke, and he kneeled next to them on the sidewalk.

Irritation flickered across Aiden's skin. He had this under control. This wasn't the first time he'd had to use the first-aid certification he'd gotten in college.

Did this guy have that? Did this guy keep it updated every year the way Aiden did?

"No. I remember him though." She tilted her head and looked at Aiden, frowning again. "I don't know from where, but I definitely know you somehow."

A familiar dread dropped heavy and low in his abdomen. The older man looked Aiden up and down before recognition lit up his eyes.

"So, are you really a doctor, or do you just play one in the movies?" A smirk spread across the guy's lips.

Aiden sighed. "I'm a personal trainer and I used to be a vet tech, so I know emergency injury procedures."

Unlike you, he added silently.

He turned back to Bree with what he hoped was a calming look. "You probably have a concussion. You should really let a doctor check you out."

"No doctors."

Did he have time to convince her otherwise? A glance at his

watch told him no, though it took effort to calm down the voice screaming in his head to haul her away to a hospital immediately.

"Fine. Can we call someone? Where's your phone?" Aiden looked around, but there was nothing on the ground.

"Someone probably grabbed it when she fell," said the other guy with a shrug.

Aiden ground his fist into the rough sidewalk. Yet another of the many reasons he hated this city. Leave your stuff unattended for two seconds and it gets stolen.

"I don't think I had one," said Bree.

"You don't have a phone?" Aiden tried to keep the shock out of his voice but did a poor job of it.

No last name, no phone, no doctors. Panic was slowly starting to take over, hot stickiness clinging to the blood in his veins. His mind searched for a solution, some plan that made sense in this totally unprecedented situation.

Instead of an enchanted fairy, maybe Bree was a demon sent to torture him. It wouldn't be the first time New York had turned something he thought was good into something terrible.

"Why don't we get you something to eat?" The older man smiled gently and got to his feet. Aiden did the same, relieved to have a next step to follow, and he reached out his hands to help Bree up.

She was unsteady, and his hoodie fell off her slender shoulders. As he bent to pick it up, he got a whiff of flowers and sugar. Her hair, maybe, or her skin. It smelled just like you'd expect a mythical creature wandering around New York without a phone to smell like.

Whatever it was, it went straight to the calming section of his brain. The anxiety took a small step back, and he could think almost clearly.

Aiden coughed, put the hoodie back on her shoulders, and moved away. "Do you know if you have any allergies?"

She scrunched up her face. "No?"

He exchanged a glance with the other man, who raised his eyebrows and named one of the gluten-free, sugar-free, organic, superfood chains that were more and more prevalent in the city these days. "I think there's one on the corner."

Aiden nodded. "No sense giving her an allergic reaction on top of a concussion."

The older man checked his watch. "It seems like you've got this under control, and I need to get to work." He hurried off before Aiden or Bree could say anything.

Aiden bit the inside of his cheek. Of course he'd be left to clean things up on his own. He didn't have time to babysit. This woman was nothing to him, just a stranger he'd happened to be near when she'd hurt herself.

Most people in the city were friendly enough, and Aiden knew if he hadn't stopped, someone else would have. But he hadn't been able to resist. The unshakable sense of duty and discipline that got him to his goals was sometimes very inconvenient.

Standing next to Bree, the phone-less fairy, Aiden found he didn't mind so much right now that he was the one who always took charge of a messy situation.

"Where's that guy going?" She turned her wide eyes to his, as if she couldn't believe someone would just walk off when someone was hurt. "Do you need to go to work too? I'm sorry, I've messed up your whole morning."

She'd messed up a lot more than that, but Aiden couldn't very well say it when she was looking at him like that. Then someone on the street rushed past, bumping into her, and sent her flying into his side.

Without thinking, he wrapped his arms around her, the sugary, floral scent overpowering whatever logical part of his brain had considered leaving her to fend for herself like anyone else would.

"Don't worry about it. I won't leave you on your own."

Read the rest in Man Of My Dreams!

Man
of my
Dreams
DAPHNE JAMES HUFF

Sweet Adult Contemporary Romance:

Houseplants and Hardcovers

Man Of My Dreams

Miller Family Medical:

A Shot At Love

Wrapped Up In You

Braced For Heartache

Wedding Games:

The Bridesmaid and the Reality Show

The Bridesmaid and the Ex

The Bridesmaid and Her Surprise Love

ABOUT THE AUTHOR

Daphne James Huff has been writing romance for adult and YA audiences since she was a young adult herself. Her favorite kind of story has a main character who thinks they've got it all figured out until someone barges into their life and messes everything up. She never says no to free cake or cheese, and can usually be found eating both to stay awake after reading all night.

Follow her on Instagram **@daphnejameshuff**